Griffin looked throug  **camera, zoomed in. H** **what he saw.**

"Looks like thousands of plants."

He could make out over forty rows with maybe a hundred plants each. Millions of dollars' worth of marijuana. But dread settled in his gut at the massive number of guards. He could sense that something was about to go south.

"Can I look through it? See what you're seeing?"

Alice had already seen some of it when she'd stumbled on it, but obviously not the vastness. "Sure, but you're not going to like it."

He handed over his superzoom camera. "Did they have that many guards when you were there?"

"I mean, men chased me. Weapons fired off—I couldn't tell how many, just that there were a lot—but now it looks like...it looks like..."

"A war zone." Packed with armed guards ready to kill.

Their little reconnaissance mission was a mistake. They shouldn't be here. Shouldn't have brought Alice. Then a man's shadow fell over him and Alice. Griffin didn't miss the silhouette of the assault rifle.

Elizabeth Goddard is the award-winning author of more than thirty novels and novellas. A 2011 Carol Award winner, she's a double finalist in the 2016 Daphne du Maurier Award for Excellence in Mystery/Suspense, and a 2016 Carol Award finalist. Elizabeth graduated with a computer science degree and worked in high-level software sales before retiring to write full-time.

Books by Elizabeth Goddard

Love Inspired Suspense

Wilderness, Inc.

Targeted for Murder
Undercover Protector
False Security
Wilderness Reunion

Mountain Cove

Buried
Untraceable
Backfire
Submerged
Tailspin
Deception

Freezing Point
Treacherous Skies
Riptide
Wilderness Peril

Visit the Author Profile page at Harlequin.com.

WILDERNESS REUNION

ELIZABETH GODDARD

HARLEQUIN® LOVE INSPIRED® SUSPENSE

Recycling programs
for this product may
not exist in your area.

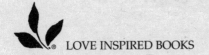

LOVE INSPIRED BOOKS

ISBN-13: 978-0-373-67834-1

Wilderness Reunion

Copyright © 2017 by Elizabeth Goddard

www.Harlequin.com

Printed in U.S.A.

There is nothing concealed that will not be disclosed, or hidden that will not be made known. What I tell you in the dark, speak in the daylight; what is whispered in your ear, proclaim from the housetops.

—Matthew 10:26-27

To Daddy. I pray for His strength, peace, love and joy as you embark on your new adventure.

Acknowledgments

Every day I wake up and thank God that He blessed me with such an amazing job—the dream job of making up stories. With God everything is possible. A journey taken alone wouldn't be nearly as fulfilling, so God has added many deep-thinking writer friends, brothers and sisters in the faith, to my life. You know who you are. I couldn't walk this writing road without you.

ONE

Danger could lurk behind the beauty. She should know that better than anyone.

Slathered in insect repellent, Alice Wilde and her client had already hiked for three days into the Oregon mountains filled with bald eagles, waterfalls and huge, winding trees—oaks, pines and junipers—while they did their best to avoid poison oak.

This was called "roughing it" by any standard.

Marie had hired Alice to lead her on a hike in the wilderness—it had been on her bucket list, she'd said. Marie had wanted this off-trail adventure far from the overcrowded Rogue River forty-mile trail and the buzzing drones in the canyon.

Tens of thousands of designated wilderness acreage still remained to explore, not counting about a million acres of Siskiyou National Forest. They weren't going to run out of places to explore anytime soon, which was something Alice loved about the area.

What she didn't love? The heat, the sweat and the bugs she'd experienced during this brutal hike. She should be in a raft guiding other enthusiasts who'd come to the region to meet the white-water rapid challenge. Except Alice had never wanted to get in that river again after what had happened eight months ago. Someone had trusted her to guide him down the Rogue River through the hazardous rapids.

Rapids that had turned deadly. The man had died on her watch.

As if her thoughts had conjured the image of flowing water, she crossed a small creek— one that eventually emptied into the Rogue River miles away. Alice followed the brook upstream. Marie continued behind her, enjoying the quiet forest as they hiked. Her feet aching, Alice would need to look for a place to set up camp for the night.

She came across a PVC pipe and froze.

Someone diverted water from this brook. Totally illegal. And a bad sign.

Glancing back at Marie who viewed the unnatural sight with curiosity, Alice warned her in a soft whisper, "Stay here."

"But the—"

Alice held a finger to her lips as she lowered her heavy pack to the ground. Pressed her palms down, signaling Marie to stay low. The woman crouched, frowning, with not a little anxiety in her eyes. Alice removed her weapon from its holster. As quietly as possible, she followed the black PVC pipe from the brook through the woods. When the pipe detoured away from the creek, she hunkered behind the thick trunk of a pine and peered through the bushy shrub growing at its base.

About a hundred yards away, through the dense forest, she could just make out an area where trees had been cut down.

Garbage—plastic bags and propane bottles—was strewn about.

And she could see the plants.

Rows and rows of plants.

Her pulse roared in her ears.

Marijuana.

Oh no!

She'd stumbled on an illegal growing operation. How big, she couldn't know. Regardless, she had to escape before anyone spotted her.

Maybe it hadn't been wise to follow the pipe, but neither would it have been wise to continue hiking without investigating. She didn't want to lead Marie into danger that could get one or both of them killed.

Now she'd need to get the global position on

her cell to mark the exact location to report to the authorities. Gripping her handgun and her cell, Alice crept backward then pivoted on her heels and ran straight into a man holding an automatic gun.

Her heart clambered behind her rib cage.

His face scrunched up. "Do I know you?"

In his fifties, silver weaved through his black hair and Van Dyke beard. Menacing dark eyes flashed at her. She'd seen him before, but where or when, she couldn't remember. Panic incapacitated every thought. No time to respond. No time to think. All she could do was act.

She whipped her weapon up and aimed at his face. He didn't seem worried in the least. She fingered the trigger and stepped sideways, giving herself a wide berth around him as she backed away from both him and the operation.

"Put your weapon down," she said.

"I don't think so."

If Alice shot him, or even fired off her weapon as a warning, she would bring the rest of the illegal operation down on her and Marie.

His eyes narrowed. "I *do* know you."

She couldn't say the same.

Alice turned and dived into the foliage, her cell slipping from her sweaty fingers, and ran. Trees and bushes scratched her face, tore her clothes, and fear that any second she'd receive a bullet to her back accosted her. A smattering of shots ricocheted off the woods behind her. The shouts of many men bounced off the trees. She didn't dare go back and retrieve her cell phone. It wasn't worth her life.

Without slowing, she caught Marie by the arm and yanked her forward. Through her gasps, she said, "We have to run and keep running, Marie. Forget the bears and rattlesnakes. There's something more deadly in these woods."

Griffin Slater downshifted to slow his motorcycle—a silver-and-blue Suzuki Hayabusa—or Busa as he called it, and the fastest motorcycle in the world. Slowing the vehicle didn't come naturally to him, but this hazardous, curvy mountain road was unmanageable at the speed he was going.

Dusk fell quickly in the woods and Griffin turned on his headlights. Two miles left before he arrived in Gideon, Oregon, in the Wild Rogue Wilderness. Weeks ago he'd contacted the sheriffs in various counties along the West Coast and informed them of his journalistic project regarding illegal marijuana grown on public land, so when his sheriff uncle called him to report a new lead, Griffin dropped everything to get there. As valuable as this could be for his story, he didn't like to think this kind of activity had sprung up in the wilderness area in his uncle's county.

The area surrounding Alice Wilde.

The fact that she'd been the one to stumble on the operation had plagued him. She could have been killed.

He'd driven in tonight because he'd wanted to get to Gideon ahead of his uncle who was coming from Gold Beach in the morning. Moisture bloomed on his hands at the thought of facing Alice for the first time since he'd walked away two years ago.

Rubbing her arms, Alice stared out the front window of her home.

You're fortunate to be alive...

Sheriff Kruse's words echoed through her. Once she and Marie had made it to a lodge where they could use the emergency radio, she'd immediately called the sheriff's department. Alice had left her pack with the SAT phone behind on her frantic run from deadly bullets. Stupid, stupid. Then someone had driven her and Marie back to Gideon and Marie left to fly home to Missouri, where she would be safe from all this mess Alice had stumbled into.

As a trained wilderness guide, she knew the

signs, knew what to look for and avoid, and yet she'd walked right into it, endangering herself and Marie. Her brothers, Cooper and Gray, would be more than furious when they found out. She didn't even want to *think* about Dad's reaction. She could almost be glad they were all out of town, but at the same time, she was terrified to be on her own.

The man in the woods claimed he knew her. Did he also know where she lived? Did her pack contain any identifying information? Then again, it probably wouldn't be so hard to find out who she was or where she lived if he didn't already know.

The sheriff wouldn't arrive until the morning. Unfortunately, he had a large county and not enough deputies to go around. Alice had a long night ahead of her. She doubted she would do more than hold her weapon, stare at the ceiling and out the windows until dawn. Might as well get out of the house while there was a little light left in the day.

Grabbing a light jacket, she left the house and headed to Ricky's Rogue Bar-B-Q. The place had practically burned down in the winter, but they'd built it back and put in a new and bigger kitchen. You could hardly tell anything had happened. At least she didn't have to spend the first part of her evening alone.

Hiking the short distance to Gideon proper took her through the woods and brought back the trauma of the last few days of running, hiking, barely sleeping as they made their way out of the wilderness to civilization.

A shiver ran through her, and she picked up her pace.

On the street, she took comfort in the still-busy small town, the familiar faces, and headed to the restaurant.

And…sensed someone following her. Or was she being paranoid?

A chilly evening breeze swept past and Alice tugged the jacket tighter.

Footsteps.

She heard footsteps behind her. She again increased her pace.

The footfalls increased as well, keeping in rhythm with her.

Then she slowed, almost stopping. The person behind her did the same.

Heart hammering, Alice wanted to look over her shoulder to see who followed her, but she knew if she saw *him*—the man she'd seen in the wilderness—fear would paralyze her.

I do know you…

Who was he? His face had been familiar somehow, but living in a tourist town and running a tourist business, she couldn't remember the name behind every face. She should turn and confront whoever followed her now. She palmed the weapon at her side, but residual fear from her narrow escape in the woods squashed her courage.

A few yards from her up the street, a figure dressed in leather stood next to a big blue motorcycle and tugged off his helmet, revealing a thick head of mussed hair. He turned and walked across the street toward her, filling her with a rush of relief. She didn't know who he was, but maybe his sturdy presence would scare her stalker away.

Bolstered, she risked a glance over her shoulder and spotted someone ten yards back watching her, his face hidden by his hoodie. Goose bumps crawled over her, and she'd learned long ago never to ignore that sensation.

She turned her attention back to hurrying across the street toward the stranger.

Though…wait. Something about his cadence seemed familiar.

No. It couldn't be.

But…it was.

Griffin Slater?

Her mind had to be playing tricks on her. She took in the broad shoulders, the trim, athletic physique. It was definitely him.

She rushed forward, putting more distance

between her and the person behind her. As she hurried toward Griffin, emotions accosted her.

Anger and resentment along with a million questions.

She could still hear the footfalls, growing closer even as she practically jogged into the street toward Griffin. She hoped to leave her shadow behind. There was safety in numbers, after all.

She stopped just short of throwing herself into Griffin's arms to find protection and comfort there. Breathing hard, she swiped a hand over her brow and stared at him. He took her in, too, and his appreciative gaze sent heat through her.

His slate-gray eyes always seemed to capture everything, just like his camera, only Griffin could see right through people, read them. Her heart pounded from her fear or from Griffin's nearness, she wasn't sure, but Alice hoped he couldn't read her right now. She wouldn't want him to know that he affected her one iota. That he'd caused an eruption of emotions, both good and bad.

"It's really you. You're not some figment of my imagination." Had she really just said those words out loud? So much for hiding her emotions.

Her knees wanted to buckle. Was that from

seeing Griffin or from yet another narrow escape from danger? She was such a coward not to face and challenge whoever had followed her, instead practically running into this man's arms.

"Yes, it's really me. Nice to see you again, Alice." His gaze briefly flicked to the town behind her.

Had he spotted the man following her? She wanted to gauge his reaction but instead she blurted out, "So you just appear out of nowhere, after two years? Why are you here?" Alice wanted to kick herself, but she couldn't help it. She wanted answers.

She risked a glance over her shoulder. The man slipped into the shadows between the buildings.

TWO

Griffin gazed into Alice's dark blue eyes. "I'll fill you in on the details, soon enough."

The wildness in her gaze had always reminded him of the way the Rogue River churned and twisted. Her eyes could always stir him up inside, like the dangerous rapids. She'd secured her light brown hair in her usual ponytail, and a few sun-kissed strands had come loose and framed her face. The smattering of freckles across her pretty nose weren't hidden beneath makeup. None of that for Alice. Another thing he'd always liked about her.

She hadn't changed a bit since the last time he saw her, except there was something different in her eyes, and he wasn't sure he liked what he saw.

This was the moment he'd dreaded and the reason he'd come to Gideon ahead of his uncle, but it was upon him much quicker than he would have liked. He'd had no time to catch his breath at the Gideon Lodge like he'd planned.

He hadn't been sure how he would feel when he faced her again, and seeing her now could bowl him over, except for the turmoil written all over her face that brought his focus back.

"What happened, Alice? What's wrong?"

She glanced over her shoulder again. So he'd read her right. There was more happening here than the anger he assumed was directed at him. Griffin fought the need to tug her to him, push her behind him, protect her. He didn't think Alice wanted that from him. And he sure didn't want the rush of unbidden feelings, but he should have expected the shock of seeing her that rolled through him.

Alice hesitated, then replied, "I think someone followed me."

"The way you say that, sounds like you mean someone might have followed you to harm you. Is that what you mean, Alice?"

"Yes, I think so, but I can't be sure. He disappeared between those buildings."

Maybe she was overreacting, but he had a feeling she wasn't. He hoped he was wrong about that. Hoped it had nothing to do with her stumbling on the illegal garden.

He started to take off in pursuit but she

grabbed his arm. "No, wait. Don't leave me. He's long gone by now anyway."

He hesitated, unsure what to do, but he didn't want to leave her alone. Plus, they needed to talk. Alice didn't know yet about his assignment, he assumed. And it sounded like there was much more about what had happened in the wilderness than Griffin knew, as well.

But before they could talk about that, he needed to address her on a more personal level. That was why he'd come. It would have seemed insensitive for him to just show up with his sheriff uncle tomorrow, especially considering how he'd left.

Three years ago, he'd come to the Wild Rogue Wilderness region to rest after a TBI—traumatic brain injury—had ended his military career and a job he lived for. After six months, he was well on his way to a full recovery and hoped to establish himself as a civilian photojournalist in conflicted regions of the world. Then…he'd met Alice. They'd grown too close, too fast.

He could still remember how she'd begged him to stay, but he'd been afraid of his growing feelings for her, so he'd taken the assignment in Kenya when an agency called looking for a freelancer. He'd assured her he would come back after the assignment and had told himself he meant it. But it had been all too easy to make excuses to never return. And now that he stood here with her, he had no clue how to bring it all up again. How to even broach the topic. Maybe Alice had moved on and had no interest in dredging it up, except her first words to him gave her away.

So you just appear out of nowhere, after two years? Why are you here?

Yeah, she wanted to talk about it.

Griffin scraped a hand down his face. He'd come to Gideon looking for her and now that he'd found her, he was tongue-tied and ashamed. He could face so many horrible things...but he couldn't let himself love someone. Why was it so hard?

"Listen, I need to head to the lodge before it's too late and make sure they have a room for me." And yet he definitely wanted her to stick with him if someone was following her. "You want to walk with me? Then we can go somewhere and you can tell me what's going on. Why someone followed you."

She nodded. "Yeah, sure." And looked over her shoulder again.

They headed off in the direction of the lodge. Dusk finally settled on the town. Griffin watched the shadows for Alice's stalker, and at the same time he tried to come up with an opening about his departure before and the fact he hadn't returned as he'd said.

Alice strolled next to him and palmed the gun tucked at her side. Wary. She was definitely wary about something.

Inside the lodge, she stepped back and waited for Griffin to check in. His call to find a room had been last-minute—risky during peak tourist season—but the woman had thought a guest planned to leave early and had said she would hold the room for Griffin.

When he announced his name, the woman paled. "I'm so sorry, sir. I thought we'd have a vacancy, but it didn't materialize. I left you a message on your cell."

Right, and he hadn't checked his messages while on his motorcycle.

"It's okay. Not your fault." Worst case he could head back to Gold Beach and stay with Uncle Davis. But he was glad he'd come, if Alice needed him.

Griffin left the registration desk to stand next to Alice, unsure what to do now. He didn't want to leave her alone if someone had followed her and she was in danger. Where were her brothers?

"You can stay in the apartment above Wilderness, Inc." Her words took him by surprise.

"What about your brother Coop? Isn't that

where he lives? Don't you think you should ask him if I can stay with him first?" Though Griffin didn't relish the idea.

"He got married. He and his wife, Hadley, live in a beautiful new cabin across town. He's out on a wilderness-training excursion, and she's off at an art show. Gray and his wife are gone, too. Wilderness, Inc. is busy in the summer. But the apartment is vacant. We keep it for guests and situations like this."

Right. Her words served to emphasize what he'd missed since his departure.

"Well, then, looks like I have no choice but to take you up on that offer."

Disappointment surged in her eyes. He'd made it sound like staying there was a last resort. Well, it kind of was. But it was still an option he was glad to have if it meant that he could stay close and keep an eye on her as she dealt with a possible stalker. And given what he already knew about her situation, he wouldn't leave her alone.

Still carrying his bag and gear, the day began to wear on him, and he knew it was far from over. She led him to the Wilderness, Inc. offices and inside the house-slash-business, up the stairs to the apartment.

He dropped his bags on the sofa and turned to face her. "Okay, so what's going on? Why did someone follow you? Who is it, do you know?"

"You first." Her expression said she was loaded for bear. "I asked you why you came back to Gideon, and you said you'd fill me in on the details soon enough. How about now?"

Griffin frowned and shrugged out of his leather jacket. Clearly, he wasn't ready to offer his explanation. But after two years Alice needed answers. She needed closure.

It had taken all of the last half hour for her to regain her composure. To control her anxiety, both over the man following her and over her reunion with Griffin—the shock of seeing him in the flesh.

And now, she wasn't sure how to tell him what she'd seen in the woods, or if she even should. She'd have to if she were to explain why someone followed her tonight.

But Griffin could give his explanation first.

Earlier, she'd just been glad to have his sturdy, protective form to walk next to in case the man she'd run into in the woods had actually followed her to Gideon, but she reminded herself she could not trust Griffin. He could disappear and leave her hanging.

Alice had always been strong and self-sufficient, but at the moment she felt weak and exposed. She wasn't sure how to get on top of this apprehension that had followed her out of the wilderness and into Gideon.

But she needed to tell him about what was going on. What had happened. So he wouldn't be taken by surprise if a bad guy showed up. It's just...she'd needed answers from Griffin first.

"Well?" she asked.

He frowned.

Would he answer her question or not?

Pulling his professional-grade camera out, he fiddled with it—his attempt at procrastination while he measured his words. And while he took his time answering, she took him in. His shoulders and biceps stretched his polo shirt, and he'd cut his shaggy brown hair to a shorter, crisp cut. He looked good. Too good, in fact, and she was sorry because that made it impossible for her to ignore her attraction to him. She shouldn't be thinking about his hair or his muscles or how good he looked.

Then his gaze snapped to hers, as if he'd known what she'd been thinking about him.

Alice couldn't hold his intensity and averted her eyes.

"I'm working with my uncle, Sheriff Kruse," he finally said. "Going into the wilderness. I'm a freelancer, documenting the increasing use of public lands to grow marijuana and covering the hazards both to the environment and to the public, especially hikers." His gaze and emphasis intensified on that last word.

Alice sagged. Deep down, she'd been expecting a much different answer. Had she honestly thought Griffin had finally come back for her after two long years? Or that his uncle had notified him of what she'd been through and he'd come running to her rescue? She plopped onto the sofa next to his duffel bag and his expensive camera case. *Of course.* Of course, he would be here for the action. This had nothing to do with Alice.

Griffin was all about action.

But, wait… "You mean your uncle called you? But why did—"

"I contacted him weeks ago along with other West Coast county sheriffs to let them in on my assignment. Let them know to contact me if they learned of any activity. I want to be there when things go down. I knew I could count on Uncle Davis to let me know if there was activity, but honestly I hadn't expected to hear from him. Nor did I want this to happen so close to him or…to you."

Weeks ago.

He'd been on the West Coast for weeks and had made no effort to contact her. Alice let those words sink in but refused to let them hurt. She had obviously thought much more of what they'd had together before than Griffin. And the importance of this situation far outweighed her pathetic actions of the past.

"He called to tell you about the marijuana farm so you could go in with him and film the whole thing?" He'd obviously told Griffin that Alice had been the one to find it, too. "But that's so dangerous. Those men don't just have guns. They have automatic weapons. They know their location has been discovered and they'll be expecting you. They're going to try to kill you, if they haven't already moved out." Alice couldn't help the dread edging her tone. She didn't want to go through losing Griffin again, though she'd never had him to begin with.

He blew out a breath, clearly frustrated. "Remember, I was a navy combat photographer. That means I was trained to operate alongside combat units in all military branches. I've worked alongside Special Forces, Alice. Documented critical missions. And now? I take on similar assignments, which you already know." He scraped a hand through his hair. "Why do I need to explain this to you? You know this. But the reason..."

Working up the courage, she finally looked

at him. His intense gaze took her in, reading her like always.

"Go on," she said.

"The reason I came here tonight ahead of Uncle Davis is that I wanted to talk to you first."

"You want to interview me about what I saw in the woods?"

"Well, that, yes, but I need to explain…about what happened before." He cleared his throat. "Two years ago."

Alice squeezed her eyes shut. Pictured herself begging him not to leave. What kind of person lowers themselves to beg? She hated that memory. She'd hated herself for the longest time after that. Still, he'd told her that he would return. And when he hadn't, she felt all the more pathetic. She'd been worried about him. It took Cooper finding out the real story from the sheriff—that Griffin was still traveling on assignment and was fine. Her brother had to break the news to her like that…she cringed inside at that memory, too. She would never let herself be that vulnerable again.

She got it. He'd only left her the reassurance of his quick return to shut her up.

At first she'd wanted an explanation from him. Now? She wanted to just drop it. "I'd prefer it if we just forget about that."

"Sure. I think that's best. But not before I apologize for behaving like I did. I didn't mean to hurt you, Alice." He frowned, hesitating as though he struggled with the words. "I'm... sorry."

His words jolted her. The regret in his gaze stripped her bare. She hadn't expected a heart-felt apology from him.

But he'd gone to Kenya.

And you never came back.

Alice definitely wouldn't say those words out loud. *Oh, why do you have to be such a great guy, I mean, to apologize, even?* How many guys were willing to accept responsibility for their mistakes?

Regrettably not many, at least that Alice had met.

"So, are we good?" He flashed his irresist-ible grin.

And she wished he hadn't. He was entirely too charming and her emotions betrayed her to respond to him like this. Still, she returned his smile and wanted to say it was so. They were good and she understood and had forgiven him. If only the pain from his departure didn't still linger. If only he wasn't sitting there again in the apartment, much too near for her. If only she could actually trust him.

"Alice?"

What kind of person would she be if she didn't truly forgive him now? Maybe the words would bring her heart along. "Yes, all is forgiven."

But not forgotten.

THREE

Hearing those words eased the weight on his heart, but they didn't erase it. She'd forgiven, but she still hadn't let it go. Obviously, he hadn't, either. Maybe neither of them would. But he'd said what he'd come to say and that's all he could do about his actions of the past.

Now might as well focus on the dangers of the present.

"Good. I'm glad to hear it. Why don't you tell me who you think followed you?"

"I think it could have been someone related to the marijuana operation."

This news wasn't good. "Tell me what happened, then."

He'd gotten his camera set up. Could use the video and record her story, which was his usual practice, but the way she looked at him now—Griffin hesitated. She'd hate it if the camera captured her looking this vulnerable and frightened. This wasn't the right time. He shut off the camera. "It's just you and me, Alice. No camera."

There. That had been the right decision. She visibly relaxed.

"But what about your uncle? He won't be mad that you questioned me before he got the details?" That soft smile again, her pretty lips a natural shade of pink.

"I guess if he wanted to be the first to hear your story, he should have gone out of his way to get here tonight like I did. But the reason I'm asking you now is because of your reaction when you rushed up to me tonight. You said someone followed you. I'm concerned for your safety, and that's not something that can just wait until tomorrow. Just tell me what happened."

Griffin tugged a handgun out and set it on the table, letting her know he'd come prepared. Then Alice spilled the details of her story and Griffin listened, never taking his eyes from her. As she relayed running through the woods with Marie, being chased by men with their weapons—AR-15 rifles converted to fully automatic assault rifles—he noticed the subtle shift in her demeanor as the terror took hold of her again.

He felt her terror as if it were his own, all the way to his marrow.

Griffin wasn't sure when it happened, but he

found himself sitting next to her on the sofa, holding her. Her soft warm form in his arms made him crazy, but more pressing was the terrifying realization that he could have lost her. Except she'd never been his to lose in the first place.

He hadn't wanted the risk to his heart, and had no claim on her.

Still.

Alice could have been killed out there.

Squeezing his eyes shut, he willed the pain of that thought away. Wasn't that the very reason he avoided getting too close to her? No one was immune to tragedy. If anyone knew that, he did.

He released her and bolted to his feet. "And you think the man knows who you are? Or was he bluffing? Trying to scare you?" That would be better. So much better.

"His face was familiar to me. Yes, I think he knows me."

The news deflated his hopes. "Knows your name *and* where you live?" But Griffin admitted to himself unfortunately that information would be easy to come by in today's world.

Alice rose and paced the small space. "Maybe."

Griffin gripped her shoulders. Forced her to look at him. "I don't want you going home. You sleep in this apartment tonight. I'll sleep downstairs in the office on the sofa." Right. He wouldn't sleep a wink. He'd keep watch until his sheriff uncle arrived in the morning. "Okay?"

She nodded, her lips spreading into a half smile. He shouldn't think about her lips. Or how perfect they were.

"Sure, okay. There's no point in lying. I'm scared to sleep at home tonight. I have my own weapon, but if several men attacked at once, it wouldn't be enough." She shuddered. "The idea of home doesn't feel safe at all anymore. Not to mention, how can I ever hike in those woods again? If I can't hike and I can't be a river guide, then what use am I to the family wilderness excursion business? I don't even know who I am anymore."

He should have said something then. Comforted her.

Instead he dropped his hands and moved to the kitchen in search of a drink. He opened the fridge and found it stocked with sodas and bottled water. He grabbed two waters and tossed her one. He'd needed the distraction so she wouldn't see his face at the revelation that she couldn't be a river guide anymore.

He'd read the news. Knew she'd guided a group down the river and lost someone. He'd known that must have upset her. But had it affected her so deeply that she hadn't gone back into the river? That had to crush her. She lived for that white-water rapid rush. Had been one of the best guides. After all, only five years ago she'd won a bronze medal in the Olympic white-water slalom, or canoe slalom as it was called. She still had it in her.

He caught her gaze and held it as they each lifted their bottled waters to their lips.

Finished, he finally said what he should have said before. "You'll hike again, Alice. And you'll take the river again. Life happens. And death." She couldn't have any idea just how much death happened. But he knew—images of war played like a never-ending reel across his mind. The impact on him was profound. And that was why he couldn't let himself get close to her.

He was a damaged man.

He grabbed his gun from the table. "Do you need to get some things from your house before you settle in here?"

Vehemently, she shook her head. "I can sleep in what I'm wearing. If he followed me to the house, I don't want to lead him here."

If they hadn't already done just that. But Griffin didn't want to bring up the possibility and scare her more than she already was. He wished her brothers were here to protect her, someone other than him. Could he be an effective protector when his heart distracted him completely whenever he was near Alice?

Regardless, and in lieu of her brothers or father, he would be here for Alice to protect her until tomorrow when the sheriff got here. She knew how to wield her weapon and on some level could protect herself, but the kind of men she'd run across in the woods were seriously dangerous.

"I just want to make it through this night," she said. "Tell the sheriff what he needs to know so he can rid the woods of the vermin and be done with it."

"Did you tell him everything? Including that the guy might have recognized you?"

She paled. "I didn't have the chance. I thought I'd have a chance to tell him more, but he had an actionable emergency and I had to wait until the morning. But now you're here."

And what if Griffin hadn't come? She had friends in town, but apparently she hadn't shared what happened with anyone. "Do Cooper and Gray even know about this? Or your father?"

"I didn't want to call Cooper or Gray. They're both on excursions and hard to reach, as it is. Dad's out of the country. There's nothing they can do anyway."

Except protect you, Alice. But it looked like Griffin was up for that job now. And wouldn't Coop and Gray just be thrilled to hear about that?

Yeah, her brothers hadn't much liked Griffin. He didn't think it was personal. Just that nobody was good enough for their sister. On some level he got that. But was she supposed to spend her life alone, then?

No. She was just supposed to pick someone better than him. Since he wasn't relationship material, why should he stick around and waste everyone's time and let himself fall for her, let her fall for him, and break both their hearts? The call to Kenya that would propel him back into action couldn't have come at a better time. Except maybe he'd broken both their hearts anyway.

Alice cleared her throat. "Imagine the reputation our business would get if Cooper cut his wilderness training short to rush back here."

She pulled out the band securing her hair and set it free, shook it out, then wrapped the band around it again, captivating his attention. A simple habit, but did she have any idea what that did to him? Her dark blue eyes blinked up at him. "And now, you're here. Thank you for showing up at just the right time."

Yeah. I'm such a great guy. I left you high

and dry and didn't come back or call, and then I happened to walk back into your life just when you needed me. I'm such a hero.

He was a coward when it came to commitment. But when it came to keeping her safe... "Nobody is going to get to you tonight, Alice." He chambered a round. "They have to go through me first."

"I don't want you to get hurt because of me."

"I've survived two tours in the Middle East, I think I'll be okay." And countless other covert missions. Griffin wanted to grip her shoulders again, make her look at him and believe him, but then again, keeping his distance was the best for both of them. "It's you I'm worried about. Now get some rest. I'll be downstairs if you need me."

He left Alice in the apartment upstairs and lay on the sofa in Cooper's office, listening. He had no intention of falling asleep, though he needed the rest to be prepared for his trek in the wilderness tomorrow with Uncle Davis and his deputies. But a woman's well-being was more important than being at his best to get the story. Otherwise what was the point?

He tried to convince himself it didn't matter that woman was Alice. And he would keep trying...

When he blinked his eyes open, he realized

that he'd fallen asleep, after all. Still, he'd been trained to sleep lightly, and a subtle sound had disturbed him, waking him.

Pressing his hand over his firearm on the side table, he waited and listened.

Had Alice moved in the apartment above? Or had an intruder approached?

Grabbing the weapon, Griffin decided to head outside to check the perimeter. The only issue he had with Cooper's old apartment was that privacy entrance in the back, which meant that someone could get to Alice without having to go past him. He grabbed a set of keys off the desk and let himself out the front door, locking it behind him.

While he wanted to wait and listen, that could be a luxury he couldn't afford. He moved around the house, quietly, and kept to the shadows.

Searching for anything out of the ordinary.

Behind the house, he waited in the shadows.

A figure crept up the stairs to the apartment.

Alice heard a noise.

Even with Griffin bunking in the office below, she hadn't been able to fall asleep. Her heart pounded at every sound, every creak of the house, hoot of an owl or cry of coyotes.

But this sound was different. The noise she'd

heard sounded close by. Maybe it was just a raccoon that snooped around, but she had to check. She palmed the grip of her weapon and peeked out the curtain, ever so carefully.

Movement on the stairs drew her attention. That was no raccoon. Nor was it Griffin.

A man dressed in dark clothing crept up the steps. So much for their grand idea that she would be safe here, and that Griffin's presence would somehow protect her. It appeared she was on her own.

A scream lodged in her throat.

Moisture slicked her hands.

Fear paralyzed her.

No. "No…" She couldn't just stand there and wait for that malicious man to kill her.

Alice shook free of the chains of terror. She would be proactive and take him out first. After chambering a round, she flung the door open and rushed through the opening, pointing her weapon out and ready to fire.

Someone shouted.

The figure on the stairs turned away from her and fired his weapon in the opposite direction. Returning gunfire from beyond him sent the man leaping down the stairs and running into the woods.

Who else was out there?

"No, don't let him get away!" she called to

whoever had chased the intruder away with gunfire.

She had to stop this. Looking over her shoulder forever was no way to live!

Fueled by adrenaline and her need to end her terror, Alice bounded down the steps. Strong arms seized her, yanking her back from her pursuit. The shock of the sudden grip ricocheted through her.

Griffin pulled her hard against him.

"Alice!" He clutched her and turned her to face him, putting just enough distance between them to get in her face. "Just what do you think you're doing?"

"I'm going after him, that's what. And you're preventing me. Now let me go."

"What? Are you crazy? You're definitely *not* going after him."

His features shadowed in the darkness, Alice couldn't see the gray in his eyes, but she could feel his gaze piercing her all the same, and she could feel the strength in the arms that had stopped her mid-run. His warmth, his presence. She calmed her breathing, let her frustration and fear slip away, and leaned into him.

Pressed against his chest she could feel his heart beating wildly like hers. Even though it was too fast, it beat strong and steady—and after a moment, the rhythm slowed, calming her.

"He might not be alone—it's too dangerous to go after him. Let's get back inside in case he tries anything else." Griffin spoke quietly, his tone not demanding, but persuasive nonetheless.

She let him tug her up the stairs into the apartment. Then watched him push the dresser out of the bedroom and shove it in front of the door to barricade it.

"Nobody's getting through that," she said.

Hands on his hips, he wiped his brow, then looked at her. "Well, that's one door, anyway."

She shook her head. "I can't live like this."

"You won't have to for more than tonight. Tomorrow everything will be over. My uncle will hike into the woods to the marijuana garden and destroy it. Catch the bad guys and lock them away."

"Tomorrow? It took Marie and me three days to hike there. There aren't any roads—you can't drive there." She had no idea if the sheriff planned to use helicopters or what, but that would negate a surprise approach and allow the criminals to scurry away like roaches and hide.

"My point is that your life will be your own again after it's over. I'm going to be here with you to keep you safe, and stand vigil until the sheriff comes in the morning. Just promise me one thing."

"What's that?"

He moved closer, his eyes peering down at her, studying, measuring. Could he read her? If he could, he knew more than she did about her own thoughts and emotions right now.

"Don't ever pull that again."

"You mean…"

"I mean running after a killer with a gun into the woods. Running after danger like that."

She thought of the moment when he'd prevented her from following, and had pulled her against him into his arms. The sound of his pounding heart, scared for her and the situation. Griffin this close to her, in the flesh…

How was it that he was in this with her now? It seemed surreal. Made her dizzy.

No, no, no… She couldn't let this man stir her like this. Even though she was grateful not to be facing this alone, it was just pure misfortune that Griffin was the one by her side—that this situation had landed him back into her life again.

"You asked if I was crazy. The truth is, I don't know why I did it. It seems pretty stupid now that I think about it, but I was determined to stop him. I can't let him torture me like this. I need to be proactive."

"Well, whether or not you had a moment of insanity, you're making *me* crazy now." Griffin grabbed and held her gently at arm's length. "Chasing after this guy just puts you in more danger. If you want to be proactive, do it by helping the sheriff catch him. You say he knew you. It would go a very long way if you can remember him. Put a name with a face."

With or without his name, her life was in danger.

FOUR

Alice woke up and splashed water on her face, ran her fingers through her hair and secured it in her ponytail. Used one of the extra toothbrushes kept at the apartment for convenience, then hurried downstairs. Men's disputing voices had drifted up through the walls into the apartment and woken her.

Rushing to meet the guys below, she bounded down the stairs to find them in the office where Griffin had stayed last night. She could see them through the window in the office door. Griffin stood next to his uncle, the sheriff, and across from the two deputies the sheriff had brought. They were caught up in an intense discussion, and she didn't think they'd noticed her yet. Seeing Griffin there unsettled her all over again. It was strange. She hesitated before entering. Rubbed her eyes and tried to shove the exhaustion away, which was pointless.

She'd been a coward when he'd apologized—

she should have asked him why he'd never come back. But she was afraid of his answer. Afraid to hear him actually say that she hadn't meant anything to him before, even though it was obvious. Now she felt like even more of an idiot for begging him not to go off to Kenya for that exposé. And for all those months after when she held on to hope he would return, or that she would hear from him again.

She had truly better forget about what happened before and let go of every unwanted emotion surrounding Griffin Slater. Once she told the sheriff everything, then he and Griffin would be off to eradicate the illegal marijuana operation—the menace to society and the danger to innocent hikers—and Alice would be done with the whole ordeal as well as with Griffin. He'd be gone for good. Again.

Drawing in a breath, she turned the knob and entered the office. All eyes looked to her—the law enforcement presence intimidating. Griffin's eyes turned dark as he held her gaze.

"Good morning, Alice. Just the person I came to see." Sheriff Kruse gestured for her to come all the way in. Funny, considering the office was hers, not his. "I want to hear everything you can tell me. What you saw and where you saw it."

With the sheriff and two deputies focused on her, her shoulders tensed.

"There's no need to be nervous. This is Deputy Reed and Deputy Edwards." Each of the men nodded. Deputy Reed was tall and skinny, like his name implied, and Edwards was average weight and height, and appeared to be in shape. Up to the task. Both men looked in their midthirties, same as Griffin. Alice had just turned thirty this year.

The sheriff pointed to a chair, and Alice took it and the steaming cup of coffee Griffin offered with a smile. She saw he'd added just enough creamer. His thoughtfulness along with his grin would normally have eased her anxiety. But she reminded herself she couldn't let down her guard. Little acts of thoughtfulness were his default. She shouldn't read too much into them and fool herself into thinking he cared more than he really did. On the contrary, she reinforced the wall she'd already built.

"Griffin filled us in on what happened last night with the man who approached the apartment. I'll get a deputy to look into it. Do you think it's related to what you saw?"

"Yes." Both she and Griffin answered.

"It had to be the man she saw in the woods," Griffin said.

"I want to hear it from Alice." Sheriff Kruse's

gaze drilled into her. His eyes reminded her of Griffin's.

She pushed those thoughts aside and focused. "Someone followed me as I walked into town last night. It happened just as Griffin got here."

"I could tell something had spooked her," Griffin said.

Sheriff Kruse sent Griffin a warning look to let Alice speak. Then his eyes shifted back to her.

"I decided not to stay in the house in case the man knew where I lived. But obviously he watched us come here and stay."

The sheriff nodded, taking it all in.

"Okay, then. Let me hear the details of what happened in the woods on your hike." Sheriff Kruse took a seat for himself and gestured for Griffin to sit, as well.

The deputies stood against the wall. Alice realized the gravity of the situation. That Sheriff Kruse had pulled two deputies from the county already strapped to focus on this. A knot lodged in her throat.

Sipping her coffee at intervals, Alice tried to remember and share every detail, while all the men listened intently. Griffin had heard the story from her last night, but he watched and listened like it was the first time.

When she finished she released a long exhale and looked at him.

Had she forgotten anything?

He gave a subtle, approving nod.

"I'm sorry to hear you believe the man recognized you, Alice." The sheriff poured himself some more coffee. "That puts you in additional danger until we take care of things. And you can't place him?"

"No, though I'm sure I've seen him before. He could have been in Gideon—a tourist, or someone who has come through Wilderness, Inc. But I can't put a name to his face."

"All things considered, I agree with your assessment the man you confronted last night could be the same man you faced in the wilderness, or at least someone involved with that operation, but we can't be sure of that. I suppose we will learn soon enough. If I recall, you guys take pictures of the groups that go out. Of your clients. Have you thought of looking through those?"

She shook her head. "No, I didn't. I guess I should have."

"Don't be too hard on yourself. You've been through a lot. When you get the chance, go through the photographs and see if you can find him."

Alice nodded. She couldn't argue with his thinking.

"What can you tell me about the marijuana garden?" he asked. "Would you say it was large or small?"

Frowning, she shook her head. "Compared to what?"

"How many rows of plants did you see?"

"I don't know. I was looking on from a distance and through the underbrush. I can't be sure, but I saw a couple of rows, at least."

"Why does it matter?" Griffin asked.

"I need to know what kind of operation this is and the exact location before I call in the multicounty task force, which would mean pulling deputies and sheriffs from several counties and possibly LEO from other agencies as well, depending on the size. Do you understand why I need to know before I bring down a storm on this location?"

"But you know that they shot at me, Sheriff. There were several men firing automatic weapons, so that tells you something, doesn't it? This isn't a minor, one-man operation."

He nodded, his expression grave. "I'm just grateful you made it out alive."

"You and me both," she said.

Griffin closed the small distance and placed both hands on her shoulders from behind, squeezing gently. Though she wanted to keep her guard up around him, through his touch she sensed his heartfelt relief that she hadn't come to any harm, and she was hard-pressed to push him away. Was it really so wrong to soak in what comfort she could get? They both knew she wasn't out of danger yet.

"There's also the chance, given how much time has lapsed since you ran into this operation, they could have pulled out already," Sheriff Kruse said.

"They could harvest before we even get there," Deputy Reed said to clarify.

Griffin shook his head. "I don't think so. They're not going to leave what amounts to millions of dollars behind. Even a small garden can add up quickly. And getting that out of those woods will take them time. It won't be any easier for them to leave than it will be for us to get there."

"True. Which brings me to this." Sheriff Kruse set his coffee mug on the desk. "We need to take the shortest and most expedient path, which isn't going to be easy in the wilderness area." He gestured to the detailed map of the region spread out on the desk. "Show me your path and the location of the operation."

Alice pointed out the path she'd taken Marie on, which really wasn't a path at all. No roads—

not even forest service roads—carved through the government-designated Wild and Scenic area. That was the whole point of a wilderness region. Disappointment curdled in her stomach at the realization of how long it would take them to get there. What if Griffin was wrong, and these men did, in fact, harvest the majority of their crops and leave before the sheriff and his crew got there? She would forever be looking over her shoulder. She couldn't trust that her life would no longer be at risk just because the operation had been shut down. They could want revenge, for all she knew. But bottom line, she had recognized that man, and would eventually remember who he was. She was a witness to his crime and he knew it.

At least…at least she wouldn't have to face those woods again for the next few days. She'd done her part by calling the sheriff and pointing him in the right direction. She dreaded that her schedule included guiding out a group next week, even though that was on the opposite side of the river. If only she could cancel, but that wouldn't be good for the Wilderness, Inc. reputation. And Alice needed to get back on the proverbial horse, at least with the hiking, or she'd lose her confidence. She had yet to get back on the river after the tragedy.

The sheriff moved to stand directly in front of Alice. Not good. Not good at all.

"Alice—" his serious tone drew her eyes to his piercing gaze "—I'm real sorry but I'm going to need you to guide us there."

"What? No!" The protector in Griffin rose up. "She showed you where she thought she'd seen the garden. That's all you need." He didn't want Alice going back into danger.

He recalled her words last night. *But that's so dangerous. Those men don't just have guns. They have automatic weapons. They know their location has been discovered and they'll be expecting you. They're going to try to kill you...* No. She couldn't do this.

Alice shrugged off Griffin's hands that he'd kept on her shoulders. "I don't want to go back in there, Sheriff, if at all possible. I'm sorry if that disappoints you, but I can't do it."

Griffin hated seeing how this ordeal had tormented Alice. He knew she was strong and resilient and she'd eventually spring back. But it was far too soon to ask this of her.

"I understand you've been through a lot, but we need an experienced guide. That's you. And you know where this garden is. You're the one to take us there, Alice, I'm sorry. Please be assured that I have no intention of getting too close or putting you in harm's way—any more than necessary."

Oh, now, those last words reassured Griffin. Not. He fumed at his uncle, and tried to push it down. He'd have words with him later.

"Can't you just swoop in with helicopters and take out the bad guys?" she asked.

"No, we can't catch the bad guys with a helicopter, especially one we don't have. Once I've identified the exact location and the details of the threat, then the task force might be able to requisition a helicopter. Regardless, I have to investigate in person first before I make that call. I don't want to waste time finding another guide, especially when you know exactly where to take us. The whole reason these guys grow weed in the wilderness is because it's hard to stumble upon. Hard to find. We could hike in the general direction and still miss it. Wouldn't you agree?"

She nodded. "You're right. You need a guide. Hiking in could be dangerous for you, and I'm the one who found the site." She folded her arms. "I just wasn't prepared to hear that from you, is all. I'll wrap my head around it and be ready."

Griffin released some of his pent-up anger. He didn't want to put Alice through this if they didn't have to. But there really was no other way. The news had upset Griffin as much as Alice. On the other hand, he understood his uncle's reasoning. It made sense. Total sense. But that didn't mean he had to like it.

"I'll be there with two of my deputies, and Griffin, who has military experience and training. We'll protect you."

Her gaze flicked to him, antagonism apparent on her features. He hoped her resistance had nothing to do with his sudden appearance and the role he played in her past.

"When do you want to leave?" she asked.

"As soon as possible, but let's think this through. Plan it out first." He pressed his finger into the map. "You said it took you three days to hike to this point. The closest forest road to that point ends here. Will that get us there any faster than your route?"

"No, it would still take days to hike from that point through the mountains. And half a day to drive the road to even get to there. The designated wilderness region is just outside of fifty thousand acres." Alice wasn't telling Griffin's uncle anything he didn't already know on that point. "The fastest way I can get you there is to take the same route Marie and I took, though it won't take quite as long since Marie and I took our time. Regardless we'll have to gear up and backpack, travel according to the water sources to refill our supply."

"That's too long, Sheriff." Deputy Edwards hiked his pants up by the belt. "There has to be a better way." He stared at Alice as though expecting her to come up with another solution.

"There is." Sheriff Kruse eyed his deputy, and then his eyes fell on Alice, his expression weighty. "The river cuts through here. If we take a raft down to this point, Bartlett Creek, and hike in from there, how much time would that save us?"

"Wait. You're asking her to guide you down the river, too?" Griffin wished he could do much more than ask a question. He wanted to shield and protect her from this whole idea, but his words could do nothing to help her.

"Yes. The river twists and curves through the mountains, but I think it could save us some time. It should be quicker that way. And the faster we get there, the better."

Griffin's anger boiled, his indignation on Alice's behalf skyrocketed. "No, Uncle Davis." His uncle didn't like him to address him personally when he was working in official capacity, but so be it. "It's enough you're making her go into the woods when she's been traumatized. But the river...just no. If it takes us three days, it takes us three days."

His uncle glowered at him, then flicked his gaze back to Alice. "How much time would this save us, Alice, if we stop off at this creek and hike in from this point?"

"It would save us almost two days, maybe a day and a half, depending on if we have to stop before we get to that point or if we run into issues on the river. But there's a problem. You'll need a special use permit to enter the wild section of the river."

"I'll clear it with the Bureau of Land Management. You've got the raft and everything we need here in Gideon to head out right now, don't you?"

Deputy Edwards shook his head. "We don't need her to guide us on a raft. We could just take a boat up the river. It would have to be a jet boat to get us over the rapids."

"I happen to know for a fact the only person who has a jet boat in Gideon is Phil Howard, my cousin." Deputy Reed scratched his nose. "And he took his boat over to Lake of the Woods for the week, which means we'd have to go all the way to Gold Beach for another one."

Sheriff Kruse glared at his man. "That's over a hundred miles up the river. It would take us all day. We'd have to start tomorrow. Using my plan, we could be where we need to be before dark tonight. Hike out before dawn and find that garden and head back. I don't want to get stuck up there near the operation after dark. It's the best way."

Alice sucked in a few breaths like she might hyperventilate. "But the river...I haven't been on the river in eight months...I..."

Griffin eyed his uncle. What was the man up to? He thought there might be three-parts truth, and one-part manipulation on his uncle's part. Was he trying to get Alice back into the river for her own good? Or was Griffin reading too much into this?

"Do you mind if I speak with Alice alone?" Griffin asked.

His uncle hesitated, obviously afraid that Griffin was about to talk her out of it, but it was just the opposite actually.

"Go ahead, but make it quick." His uncle held the door for the deputies. "We'll be outside. I need to talk to my deputies, anyway."

Once they were alone, Griffin wasn't sure what he would say. But he had to somehow talk her down. If Uncle Davis insisted on using Alice, then the very least Griffin could do was instill confidence in her that she could handle this. It might make the difference between life and death. "Look, I don't like this any more than you do."

"I don't think you understand. Just the

thought of it gives me panic attacks. I wasn't the one to drown, but I wake up with cold sweats at night even now from what happened." Again Alice gulped for air.

He handed her a paper sack he found in a drawer. "Here, breathe into this."

She took it eagerly. Inhaled and exhaled into the bag.

"You're the best chance we have of getting there, Alice. You're the best wilderness guide, the best river guide, regardless of what happened before."

He tipped her chin up and looked in her eyes. His throat grew thick. Maybe he wasn't the one to persuade her, but he couldn't let his fear of getting close to her again get in the way. He needed to persuade her that she was still the best.

"You know how to get us there, where you're going, where to take us. You're the sheriff's best chance of finding and stopping this illegal activity. The whole reason I put myself in harm's way to get my stories is to shine a light in the dark places. To help right the wrongs in this world. To save people. To save animals and the land, the environment. If people like you and me don't stand up for what's right, don't take a stand against people like these men growing marijuana, destroying ten acres for every one acre of pot they grow, then the problem can only get worse. Only get bigger."

As he said the words, he watched the increasing anxiety in her face. A crushing sensation grew in his chest as a vise squeezed. Was he doing the right thing in convincing her?

God, please help me.

She averted her gaze and stepped away. "I need time to think it through."

He was certain that self-doubt had to be the only thing standing in her way. The Alice he knew from before would be all over taking these guys down. If nothing else, Griffin had to encourage her.

"Everyone knows you're the best white-water rapid guide there is. Everyone except you. What happened before was tragic, yes. Bad things happen to people all the time. I should know. I've spent my career taking pictures of those bad things." His tone grew dark. Anger infused him at the atrocities. "We have a chance to stop this before someone else gets hurt. We can't let this go on even one more day longer than necessary. And I promise…"

What was he doing, promising anything? He was the one afraid of commitment of any kind.

Her dark blues blinked up at him, hanging on his last words. "You promise what?" Her tone suggested she wouldn't believe anything he said, and why should she?

He swallowed. "I promise I'll protect you." *With my own life, if necessary.* "You don't have to worry. All you have to do is guide us."

He hoped his words would mean something to her, would convince her. Something shifted behind her gaze. And he read the message easily enough. A message he deserved.

She didn't trust him.

FIVE

They headed east traveling around the wilderness region to their entry point at Grave Creek. The road twisted and turned as they drove through the mountains on the north side of the Rogue River at what felt like a snail's pace, inching around every bend in the sometimes one-lane road until they came to a four-wheel drive emergency road. This would get them to the lodge with a boat ramp—and then they'd start the Wild and Scenic portion of the river.

Riding in the sheriff's department SUV with Sheriff Kruse, Alice sat in the backseat, letting Griffin sit shotgun with his uncle. The two deputies followed in another vehicle crammed with the rest of the equipment and their supplies—food and water, extra clothes, limited weapons and ammo due to weight restrictions—all packed in waterproof gear bags, and the inflatable raft she'd guide using the bigger oars, and then the smaller paddles the others would use to assist. Rafts weren't as agile as regular boats but were safer in the rapids. A drift boat would capsize too easily.

Alice still couldn't believe this was actually happening.

She'd agreed to do this. She'd known she would, eventually, but Griffin had been the one—oddly enough—to talk her down. To help her see that she remained one of the best guides on the Rogue River. Not that having the best mattered to the sheriff's department when she was immediately on hand and was also the one who knew where to lead them, where to guide them to the illegal operation.

Still, as Sheriff Kruse turned the sharp corner on the gravel road that led them closer to the boat ramp on the river, Alice wished she'd called her brothers to tell them everything that had happened. They would have come back and been there to once again overprotect her. It surprised her, too, that the sheriff hadn't called Cooper himself. Maybe he knew her brother would never have agreed to let her go.

But Alice didn't need the protection. She was a grown woman, experienced in what mattered here, the best at what she did. Certified as a wilderness first responder, CPR and swift water rescue, and she knew this river like the back of her hand. Loved every twist and turn, every pool, stream and waterfall as well as the history to go with it. Though terrified, a small thrill ran through her—she was actually getting back on the Rogue River.

She hated to admit it, but Griffin's encouragement had meant a lot. Maybe even made the difference. She could almost wish he hadn't disappeared from her life to begin with.

But he had.

End of story. She wouldn't let herself fall for him now that she understood he wasn't the right kind of person for her—something her brothers had seen all along. On the drive, he and Sheriff Kruse carried on a long conversation about Griffin's exploits and world travels in his journalistic efforts to expose the wrongs in the world—which left her to herself.

Fine with her. The closer they got the more the doubts crept back in, despite her earlier courageous thoughts. She stared out the window and fought the nausea roiling in the pit of her stomach. Tried to compose herself and get her act together. Their lives depended on her.

I can do this.

When the vehicle stopped at Grave Creek near the boat ramp, the sheriff got out. Behind them, the deputies also climbed from their vehicle. But Alice remained where she sat. Griffin, too. A slight tremble started in her legs and quickly worked its way up to her arms and finally her lower lip. Griffin turned around to face her and reached between the captain seats. He slipped his hand over hers and squeezed. She looked up at him.

"You're going to do fine, Alice." He shot her that cute, disarming grin of his. "Remember, we're not inexperienced at this. We've all been down the river before. It's fun and games for most people out there. Keep your focus on the prize—taking these men down." He gave her one last squeeze, then stepped from the vehicle.

She liked that he always knew when to give her space. Even though she didn't fully trust him, at least he knew her that well. But it was easy for him to say the encouraging words. Far different for her to live them out. The thought of their mission sucked all her bravado away and could paralyze her if she let it.

Alice released a long exhale. "Showtime."

They inflated the raft, loaded the packs and gear, food and water, their small stash of weapons and ammo, and Alice secured the paddles and most important the oars she would use to guide them. They geared up with helmets and life jackets to be safe.

God, please don't let me panic. Please don't let me seize up. Please let me guide the sher-

iff and his men to the guy I saw and his marijuana. Let us get in and out safely.

The raft positioned and anchored in the water, Alice stood on the bank. Wide and wild, the Rogue River rushed past her, and she breathed in the familiar smells of nature—a clear and pristine rushing river, the boulders and fish and musty loam. Memories, both bad and good, swirled around her, tumbled over her like she'd been caught in the rapids. She couldn't stay caught in the maelstrom of the past.

Everyone looked to her—she was their guide, after all. Heart pounding, she gave the signal and they climbed onto the raft. Alice sat in her position at the back and gripped the oars.

Her pulse jumped.

With so much riding on her, she didn't have time to be scared. That was good.

Alice focused her attention, running down her mental checklist.

Breathe in. Breathe out. And just keep going.

She worked the oars, easing the raft away from the bank and into the current, working her way, egressing out to the center of the river. Nothing bad usually happened in the middle. It was the riverbanks with the sweepers, logs and rocks that were the issue.

The river took hold of the raft, and she had the distinct impression she no longer had control over her life. But that wasn't true. That was only her fear getting in the way. The river might fool others, but Alice knew how to tame the beast. She always had, and she let the thrill of being on the river again—after eight excruciatingly long months—wash away thoughts of the tragedy. When she spotted Griffin studying her, gauging her, she heard his silent question loud and clear.

Are you okay?

Did he truly care or was he only concerned for his own skin? The question of his sincerity aside, she couldn't help it—she beamed at him, and in return he smiled back, admiration in his expression. Real appreciation. It warmed her heart more than she would like. She shouldn't care if he admired her. But it seemed he'd never lost confidence in her. Too bad she had lost confidence in him. Still, she couldn't think about any of that.

The river could make them or break them, and they still had so far to go even once they made their point of entry into the wilderness where they would hike out. If they missed that entry point somehow and went too far down the river, they'd have to travel to the end of the Wild and Scenic portion because there was no way they could simply hike out—too many canyon walls to climb.

They had one shot.

That's another reason why the sheriff had insisted on Alice as his guide, she was sure of it. Unfortunately, their route meant taking them through Blossom Bar and the Picket Fence where she'd lost a man, but she reminded herself just how many times she'd done that before the accident. She'd won a medal in the Olympics, for crying out loud. She'd just keep building up her confidence. It wouldn't do for her to dump the sheriff, two deputies and Griffin in the river, or end up with someone drowning again while Alice guided them.

Everyone appeared energetic and focused on the river and obtaining their goals as they entered the Mule Creek Canyon and hit Class III rapids at the entrance. She shouted out instructions so the men could use the extra paddles and assist in maneuvering the currents created from the rock walls on either side, and avoid the boils, then another Class III rapid within the canyon.

Once they were through the rapid, she should have been exhilarated but her palms grew sweaty as her anxiety increased.

Blossom Bar was next. She'd lost someone there…

Griffin shot her a glance. Nodded and gave her a thumbs-up, then palmed his paddles. She refused to release her oar but gave him a subtle nod in return. What choice did she have? They had to face the rapids like everyone else. Like she had, so many times in the past.

As they approached Blossom Bar, the roar of her pulse grew louder than the roar of the rapids. It was a churning Class IV rapid, not even as challenging as the Class V they'd yet to face. Boulders lined up on one side and could snag them. Those were called the Picket Fence. That's where the problems could arise. People had died there.

Seven in one year. One on her watch.

If she could make this, just make this, she might be free of her terror forever. The men held on to their paddles to assist her, but she wasn't sure she wanted their help. Might be easier to go this alone in case someone misunderstood which direction they needed to go and put them in the boil. She couldn't see Sheriff Kruse's eyes behind his sunglasses, but she had the distinct impression he watched her like a hawk even as he focused on the furious water around them.

She didn't have time to worry as the rapids caught them up, splashing and soaking them where they sat in the raft. Alice worked her oars and avoided the rocks, guiding them through.

"It's all good, Alice." Griffin dug his paddle in. "We're doing this."

"We're going to the left of the big boulders first, then we'll have to make a quick right. We want the line of rocks called Picket Fence to our left. Everybody got that?"

The men focused on the river as she guided the raft through the rapids around the large boulders.

"Now! Right, keep to the right. We're approaching Picket Fence. Need to catch that eddy before the rocks." She shouted over the roar of the rapids, hoping the men would follow through or not paddle at all. The hole on the other side of the line of rocks could suck them in and never let them go.

When the raft rushed past the boulders of the Picket Fence, they all whooped and hollered as if they were tourists on the river for fun, which couldn't have been further from the truth.

Still, Alice felt a measure of pure elation, and she wanted to share it with Griffin. Why, why, had her thoughts gone to him first?

Holding his paddle, Griffin pumped both his arms in the air. "You did it, Alice. I knew you could!"

She didn't respond, but couldn't hide her response when hearing his words made her smile even bigger. She continued to work the oars, preparing for the next set of rapids, Devil's Staircase. After that, their stop—their point of entry into the wilderness—would be up ahead where the canyon opened up. The last rapid was minor compared to the deadly stretch she had just guided them through.

Then gunfire echoed through the canyon, bouncing off the walls. Her heart rate spiked. Alice jerked her gaze up, fear crawling over her. That hadn't been meant for her, had it? Or for them as a group?

But she had no time to worry about that and quickly refocused on the approaching rapids and falls. Except she was the only one. The men stared up the walls of the canyon and moved from their positions. Sheriff Kruse had dropped his paddles and held his weapon out and ready.

"Focus, people! Hang on!" she called.

Another shot rang out.

Oh, God, please help us! How could this be happening?

The raft tilted and swirled as it carried them, tumbling over the rapids even as Deputy Edwards grabbed his arm and fell out of the raft and into the water. At the same moment, the raft's balance shifted on the rapids, the white water lifted it on one end, dumping everyone into the river with Deputy Edwards.

SIX

Who had shot at them? What was going on?

A woman's scream mingled with men's shouts, bombarding Griffin from all sides. Cold pervaded him as his body hit the white water, submerging completely, the current snatching him up and rolling him like a hungry crocodile. The boiling rapids sucked him under, the roar drowning out every other sound, filling his ears, his mind, his world, turning and twisting him. Even with his life vest, it took far too long before he breached the surface.

Heart hammering, lungs screaming, nose burning, he sucked in air and water. Coughed and fought for more oxygen and less river in his mouth and lungs. But that wasn't all he had to worry about.

Deputy Edwards had fallen out of the raft before they'd all been dunked. He'd been shot. Griffin was sure of it and had to find the deputy, he had to find Alice. How would the deputy survive the river if he'd been injured? And with Alice's anxiety over this journey, she could be in the throes of a panic attack right now, unable to get herself to safety.

The canyon still loomed above them, but he saw no one there holding a weapon or aiming at them. A millisecond before getting dunked again, Griffin spotted the injured deputy and called out to him. Concern for the others rippled through him even as he fought for his own life.

Alice...she hadn't wanted to get back in this water. He'd done this to her.

"Griffin!" she shouted.

Did she need him? He started to make his way toward her. If he could just get close to her, then together they could ride this out. But the rushing river overwhelmed him, the rapids pulled him under. Water accosted his face.

His life jacket yanked him back to the surface, where he bobbed along and hoped the water would begin to calm, to smooth out. Another gunshot rang out. At the sound, his heart rate jumped even higher.

Three shots in total. Had anyone else been hit? Would they pick them off like ducks on the water?

God, please help us. Keep us safe! Keep Alice safe...

He remembered his training regarding surviving the river. On his back, feet first, was what he'd been told. Let the current carry him. But that could take him away from the others and he had to find the deputy again. Had to make sure Alice was okay. That she hadn't been shot.

Ahead, beyond this section of white water, the river smoothed out. Griffin caught sight of Alice, Sheriff Kruse and Deputy Reed. The raft was getting away.

"Go…go get the raft. I'll get Edwards!" He shouted above the swooshing din of the river.

Alice nodded and the sheriff and Reed joined her in swimming toward the raft to retrieve it for them all. Griffin was closer to the deputy and swam forward until he reached him. Deputy Edwards was swimming with his one good arm, which wasn't very effective. Relief washed over Griffin that the man hadn't drowned. But there was still the matter of the gunshot wound.

"I got you." Griffin grabbed the man and started swimming toward the only bank he could see downriver which was closer to them than the raft at the moment.

"I'm okay," the deputy said. "I can do it."

"Are you shot?" Griffin thought so, but wanted to confirm his suspicions.

"Yeah, and it burns like fire, but I think it's only a graze. A flesh wound."

"In this cold, numbing water you can't know for sure how bad it is. We'll take care of it as soon as we get to the riverbank."

Deputy Edwards coughed up water. He'd taken more river than air in, looked like. Griffin was glad he'd gone to help, and continued swimming, assisting the deputy as he talked with the man, gasping for breath between words, until finally, they could both stand up in the calmer water of an eddy by the riverbank. They were near the end of the canyon now.

Griffin looked at Edwards. His form trembled as he pressed his left hand against the right side of his arm and shoulder. Griffin wasn't sure where the man had been shot. Edwards glanced at him, relief washing away the raw fear in his gaze.

"Thanks for that. Thanks for helping me get out of this river."

The raft dumping them like that at such a dangerous point in the river had shaken them all.

Alice...

What would this do to her? Would it shake her confidence again? Stir up her self-doubt? *God, please no.* She'd done so well and the raft tipping had nothing at all to do with her skills.

Griffin assisted Edwards all the way onto the shallow beach. Together they plopped on the gray sand and peered out at a river that was oblivious to the lives it could make or break. He could see that his uncle, Deputy Reed and Alice had all climbed back into the raft. She was safe as were the others. Dripping wet and shaken but safe.

Griffin turned his attention to Deputy Edwards's gunshot wound while Alice rowed toward them on the riverbank. "Not much we can do until they get here with the medical supplies, but looks like you're right. Bullet grazed you but it's deep. Maybe tore some muscle there."

He put pressure on the man's arm to give him a rest.

Edwards winced, gritting his teeth. "Like I said, hurts. Feels like fire burning through me."

Alice and the other two men hopped out and secured the raft. His uncle and Deputy Reed approached. Uncle Davis held the medical supply kit. Griffin explained the damage and left Edwards in their hands. He glanced up the canyon walls. They'd drifted around a twist in the river. Whoever had shot at them before couldn't get to them now. That had been a trying few minutes, but he prepared himself for another trial—reassuring Alice if she needed that.

He released a long exhale as he made his way

over to her where she stood at the raft, and he could see something was clearly wrong with Alice. And the raft…

Picking up his pace, he rushed to her side. "What is it? What's wrong?"

"A bullet punctured the raft." Her voice sounded frantic. "Get me the supplies now. I can tape it off. We can pump some air back into it."

Fortunately, the supplies sat low and had remained secured in the raft, unlike the raft's passengers. After scrounging through a few boxes, he finally found the needed supplies to repair the raft. They had to work hard and fast before they lost too much air. Alice taped the puncture and Griffin used the pump to fill the raft back up. Wouldn't do to get stuck here without a functional watercraft. They needed the raft intact to exit the Wild and Scenic portion of the river once they'd finished their surveillance. With the hole taped over and the raft filled back to capacity, Griffin released an audible sigh. And, he'd found the bullet that had done the damage, but he kept that to himself. He'd show his uncle later.

"That was cutting things close." He eyed Alice's handiwork and hoped that would be enough to get them the rest of the way.

"Too close." She rubbed her arms, her gaze

also skimming the area around them. She nodded toward the deputies. "He going to be okay?"

"I think so, yes. Lost some blood, but it wasn't serious. It could have been so much worse."

She locked eyes with him. Not a little fear swam in her gaze. What else was she thinking?

"I can't believe they shot at us, I mean, if it's the same guy, the same group of men."

He shrugged. "Who else could it be? You don't have anybody else out there who wants you dead, do you?" He so wished he hadn't said that.

"Not that I know of." Anger flashed in her eyes. "Do you? You're the one who goes around trying to expose bad guys. Maybe it's someone after you."

"Come on, you know I didn't mean it like that. What I meant is that we know someone is after you, either to kill you or at least prevent you from leading the law back to them."

She glared at him.

Griffin, could you be any more insensitive? "Okay, I'm just going to be quiet now."

"Good idea," she said, softening. "We all need to take a few minutes and gather our wits."

She rolled her neck around and rubbed it, the stress, the pressure of being hunted by these men and heading right back into their lair getting to her. Griffin wanted to close the distance to comfort her, but by the look on her face, she would have rejected his efforts anyway.

Instead, he took off his life vest. Let the sun warm and dry him out. A glance over to the others told him Uncle Davis was still examining his deputy's arm. Next to him, the small emergency medical kit sat open. Griffin needed to talk to his uncle about this risky operation and Alice's safety. He approached the men.

Deputy Edwards looked up at him, a pained expression on his face. "You helped me get to shore. I'm not sure I could have made it. I didn't want to go rafting to begin with in case the worst-case scenario happened. I'm not that great of a swimmer."

"You were doing well on your own considering you only had one good arm."

"And a life jacket," Edwards said.

Deputy Reed snorted. "Good thing there aren't piranhas in that river with all the blood to attract them."

Wow. They were all letting the wrong words slip through.

"Thanks for that." Edwards lay flat on the beach and closed his eyes.

Now was Griffin's chance to speak to his

uncle. "I'm concerned about our safety. About Alice's safety."

"And we'll talk about that soon enough, but we have no choice but to keep going. And that girl's going to need some encouragement." His uncle gestured to Alice, the message on his face clear. He wanted Griffin to be the one to reassure her.

He nodded, but let his incredulity at this predicament roll over him and reflect in his gaze.

Approaching her again, Griffin lifted a hand. Wanted to touch her. To connect. Ask if she was okay. But he thought better of it. She was much better equipped, personally, than any of them to deal with these situations. Had all the qualifications. Wilderness first responder, CPR and certified in swift water rescue. Stronger, when it came to the river, too. One of the best in the world, if winning a medal in the slalom white-water rapids at the Olympics counted. Who was he to reassure her, really? And yet, he understood she'd been psychologically crippled.

Still, he'd try a different tack as he watched her rifle through her waterproof bag for dry clothes. "So I got my wits about me this time."

"Oh? You got something more to say, then?"

"Yes. Yes, I do."

"Go on." Alice appeared to only half listen as she pulled out a T-shirt and examined it, but

Griffin knew she was trying to distract herself from her fear and pain.

"We made it through. You brought us through, Alice. Like I said before, you're the best."

"Right. We got dunked. Someone could have drowned."

"Not your fault. Someone shot at us, knocking things off balance. Knocking the raft itself off balance with that bullet puncture. Drawing our focus away at the worst possible moment. You had no control over that." Griffin eyed the canyon surrounding them for the hundredth time. Would the shooter follow and try again? Were they safe here in this small cove near the end of the canyon?

"Doesn't matter whose fault it is. We're behind the sheriff's timeline now. We need to camp here tonight," she said. "It's too late to take the river again. We lost too much time when we went into the water. Rafting was a bad idea."

Yeah, well, like his uncle said, they were here now and it was a moot point. Funny how hard she concentrated on finding the right T-shirt between the two she'd brought. "How much farther to our exit point?"

"A few miles more but we won't make it before dark. What does your uncle want to do now? Keep going?" A set of dry clothes in her hands, she closed her bag and straightened, her tenuous expression searching the lofty ridges around them and probably not for the last time.

They were stuck with those ridges until they got farther down the river. "You're the guide, we go with what you say."

"What I would say only applies under normal circumstances. Here, hold these." She handed her clothes over to him and released the band from her damp hair, weaving her fingers through. Wincing as she worked through the wet tangles.

Griffin wanted to help her with her hair, with the tangles. He shoved that impulsive thought out of his mind. "I think you're right, we should stay here for the night. By the time we get back in the water, it'll be too late. But how far will that put us behind his schedule?"

Finished working out her tangles, she didn't restrain her hair again but left it loose, presumably to dry. "We won't be hiking at dawn like he wanted, but by midmorning at least."

She eyed the river, wariness in her gaze.

"What's wrong?"

"I think we could be ambushed here."

Her troubled blue gaze roamed the rock walls around them and then settled on him. He hated that he was adding to her distress, yet throughout all of it, Alice had a stiff upper lip. Refused to show any weakness while she was in her element. Griffin liked that about her, but on the other hand, he couldn't help but think about last night when he'd prevented her from chasing the man who'd approached the apartment under cover of darkness. She ignited his protectiveness when she'd leaned into him. Needed him. And he'd needed to feel her in his arms then.

Their hearts had pounded together.

The strong urge to be close to her again surged through him. Wrong. Just wrong. He steeled himself against those unbidden emotions running through him and ignored what he wanted and needed. It could never be. Still. They'd had an emotional connection once. And he realized now that it had never truly gone away. He and Alice were inexplicably connected. He couldn't let that grow, but how did he cut loose, especially since this wasn't the time to try and sever that connection? He was beginning to wonder if he had any choice when it came to his feelings for Alice.

"Why don't you get some rest. Get something to eat. I'll talk to my uncle." Again.

Alice nodded. "Why don't you guys set up the tents first, then I'll get some rest."

Griffin chuckled. He left her and approached his uncle who stood with Deputy Reed. They had walked the perimeter of the small cove, checking things out, maybe thinking through their limited options.

"How is she?"

"She's fine on the surface, same as the rest of us." He held up the bullet for his uncle's and the deputies' eyes only. "I found this. It punctured the raft in two places. A .308. Could be used in any number of sniper rifles. What do you think? Are we sitting targets here?"

His uncle's frown deepened as he took the evidence. "Between you and me, I think that first shot was meant for Alice."

Griffin's gut tensed. He hadn't wanted to hear that. "What makes you say that?"

"The angle and trajectory. With the rapids shifting the raft, the bullet missed her and grazed Edwards."

Griffin wasn't sure Alice was the target. Why kill her now? After all, the man could have shot her last night, then made a run for it. What was going on? "And when he missed, maybe the second and third shots were meant to slow us down. Maybe he targeted the raft to make that possible, or he missed."

"Why put a sniper up at the top of that canyon if he wasn't any good at his job?" Reed asked.

Uncle Davis angled his head in thought.

Griffin finally broke the silence with the question they all had to be thinking. "Whatever the intention, how was any of it even possible? How could they have known we'd be here? How could they have followed us?"

"How could they have known we'd take the river?" Edwards piped up from where he rested on the sand, nursing his wound.

Frown lines creased his uncle's forehead. "All I can assume is that someone waited up on the ridge for us. I don't know how they knew we'd be here. Maybe they have other men waiting at the other routes we could have taken."

Dread curdled in Griffin's stomach. This situation was far more dangerous than he could have anticipated. These men were smart.

"They might have more people watching along the way to take Alice out if she tries to lead someone back," Reed added.

Unpleasant, disrespectful words rose up, but Griffin shoved them down. "All the more reason she shouldn't be here."

"What are you suggesting?" His uncle's voice rose. "That we abort?"

"That's exactly what I'm suggesting. Call in the cavalry. You have to know by now this is a big operation. Someone shooting at us confirms that. Call in your task force."

"I agree it's time to make that call to alert

them to assemble," his uncle said, "but I can't make any calls in this canyon. I'll reach out as soon as I can. Let them know to prepare the task force. It'll still take them time to pull the resources, and in the meantime, we'll be hiking in to confirm the location and what we're up against."

Griffin clenched his fists. "But they're expecting us."

"Don't tell me you're scared." His uncle chugged from his bottle of water.

"Not for myself, but for Alice."

"Look around you. These are big woods. Whoever shot at us was waiting deep in the canyon, a few miles back. He has to climb out, in fact, to warn his buddies. That'll take him some time."

"Unless he has a radio or a SAT phone, but don't you get it?" Griffin asked. "A warning might not even be needed if they have people positioned all over, waiting for their own chances to take a shot." He thrust his hand through his hair. "I don't like this, Uncle Davis."

"Look, nobody is that good. They can't be out there guarding even a small fraction of tens of thousands of acres of wilderness area for their operation. That defeats the purpose of setting up in such a remote region. That's another reason why we're taking the river. We'll take the only exit point before the next set of rapids and we'll find this operation. We're not turning back now."

His uncle continued to deflect his arguments and Griffin rapidly deflated, much quicker than the bullet-punctured raft. "Why didn't we just use a jet boat, Uncle Davis?"

His uncle eyed him, squinting one eye. "It was my call, son. I used what was most expedient and what was available. Now we're almost there and it's a moot point."

Griffin kicked hard at the sand. He thought he'd wanted that story, but all he cared about, all he could think about now was Alice's safety. He didn't want to let himself care so much. Didn't he know better? But he couldn't take it if she were to get hurt. How did he convince his uncle?

A group of kayakers floated by, having made it through the rapids, and released a loud, celebratory brouhaha. They probably had plans to stay at the lodge farther down.

Griffin would give it one more shot. "Our next attacker could get to us here in this cove before we head out in the morning."

"We'll keep watch tonight, there's no doubt there."

"Let me take her back after we reach our

drop-off point," Griffin pleaded. "We'll take the raft and head down the river. You and your deputies can keep going. I'll send a boat back for you."

"No." Alice stepped up. "If we're going to find these guys and take the operation down, the sheriff needs me to guide him. I'm their best chance. We're already here. I can't spend the rest of my life wondering, looking over my shoulder." She directed her next words and the fire in her gaze at Griffin. "I'll admit I was scared before. I didn't want to come, but I'm beyond that now. I'm just plain mad. These guys shooting at me on *my* river. You hear me? *My* river? I'm not going to let them get away with it. Now let's set up the tents and eat. I'm hungry. We'll head out first light."

Alice walked away without waiting for their reply.

And then Griffin's sheriff uncle looked at him, the small victory evident in his features. "You have to admit she's a strong one, your Alice. All she needed was a little push back into the water."

His uncle's words set him fuming again. Was this really the way to go about helping Alice over her fears? His uncle headed over to assist her and Deputy Reed with the tents, and left Griffin standing there.

Your Alice...

* * *

Later, when darkness had settled and the law slept in tents, Griffin stayed up, watching and listening. Guarding their camp for his shift. Alice should be sleeping, resting for tomorrow but instead she sat next to him by a small fire. "I'm sorry I talked you into this." He shook his head, cringing inside. "I made a mistake. Please…just, let's go back. Let me take you back. You don't have to do this anymore." He was the one begging this time for far different reasons.

She chuckled, her face soft in the firelight, hair hanging down, spreading over her shoulders. "I'm sorry. *You're* going to take *me* back? I think you have that backward."

He realized what she meant. "Right. You're the guide here. Well, how about you take me back, then? We'll figure out another way to get these guys."

"If the man I ran into hadn't recognized me, I'd say sure. Let's find another way. But he did. I'm the witness to his crime. And I'm in danger of retaliation whether I go to the garden or not. I have to be proactive or he'll find me again. You get that, don't you? Going back isn't an option for me anymore. Go back to where? Where could I go to be safe?"

He nodded. "Yeah." He didn't recognize his

own voice. And unfortunately, yeah. He got it.
God, there has to be another way...

Using a small stick, she played with the fire,
stirring up the embers, then angled her head
at him. Beautiful. Alice Wilde was absolutely
stunning in the firelight. Her natural look, her
toned arms and body fit perfectly in this wilderness on a crazy river. And her heart—she
had the heart of a wild mare who would endure
until the end, even if it killed her. Who, without even trying, dared Griffin to catch her if
he could.

His mouth went dry. Nothing new when it
came to his reaction to her. But why couldn't
he successfully bury that away forever?

Brain scrambled, he didn't know what he was
doing when he lifted a hand, swept the soft ten-
drils of her hair back and touched a thumb to
her smooth cheek. "You're beautiful."

She rewarded him with a sweet smile. "Why
didn't you come back to Gideon?"

Did it really matter anymore? He was here
with her now. He had reasons he'd left. Reasons he hadn't come back. Important reasons.
What were they again? For the life of him he
couldn't remember. "I don't know."

With Alice filling his head—her nearness,
her scent, rocking his world again—he couldn't

remember the reasons. But he remembered one thing.

When this was over, he couldn't stay.

SEVEN

Hours passed and, sitting alone as he guarded the camp for his shift, Griffin nearly drifted to sleep, could hardly keep his eyes open. That disturbed him. He'd been trained to stay awake and alert for as long as necessary, or at the very least a few extra hours. What was wrong with him? Maybe his traumatic brain injury had messed him up in more ways than one.

The small fire slowly died and he stirred it. Good thing he could hear someone moving around in his uncle's tent. It was almost time for the shift change, and then in a few hours morning would be there and they could start all over on what was turning into a nightmarish mission.

He stood to his feet to shake off the sleep until his time to stand guard had ended. The fire flickered back to life, shadows danced against the rock walls and up in the trees.

The hair on the back of his neck stood up.

That sense someone watched them pinged through him. He stood stock-still and listened. A pebble trickled down the cliff wall. Griffin hurried behind a boulder and watched the shadows, wishing he hadn't built up the fire that made him easy for anyone watching the camp to see.

He could go for some military-grade night vision goggles about now. But someone was hiding in the shadows, he sensed that much. He crept deeper into the darkness, outside of the circle of light where their tents had been set up. His uncle would be coming out of his soon and would be an easy target. He hoped he could find whoever stalked them before it was too late. But he didn't want to shout a warning and lose the guy. He had to catch him now so they would have one less thing to worry about. One less person after Alice.

He sensed the moment when someone crept up behind him. He turned to face the glint of a knife and was relieved of his gun before he could use it. Reflex took over as he fought the intruder. He disarmed the man but not before receiving a painful slash across his temple. It burned like fire—just like Edwards's gunshot wound. The warm blood leaked into his eye and half blinded him. But still he fought, until they found themselves at the river's edge.

Griffin freed himself from the man's constant punches long enough to reach for his own knife and pressed it firmly against the man's neck.

"Why are you here?"

"To stop you if you tried to find us. To stop her if she tried to lead you."

Nothing he didn't already know. "Who do you work for?"

When he didn't answer, Griffin drew blood with the knife. "I'll kill you, I'm warning you."

The man spit in Griffin's face. Knowing Griffin had been temporarily distracted, the man tried to shove the knife away, tried to escape. But the struggle just made Griffin press forward with the knife, and the man ended up walking right into it. His body dropped into the water and floated away, leaving Griffin standing there, holding a bloody knife.

His uncle rushed up behind him.

"Griff, son, what happened?"

"I killed him."

"Who was it?"

Frowning, he watched the river take the body. Griffin had no plans to go chasing after it. It would be found down the river, hopefully by those who searched for it, but more likely by the wrong people—families riding the river to experience life. He blew out a breath and shrugged.

"One of the guys after Alice. I don't think it was the man she saw, though. He didn't have the beard she'd described. I think it was just a low-level henchman. Someone sent to stop us. He dropped his weapon over there." Griffin led his uncle to where the fighting had started and picked up the weapon. Looked it over.

His uncle swiped a hand down his face. "I hate being trapped like this. I know taking the river was my idea, but I hadn't counted on things going wrong like this. I'll need to call everything in as soon as I can communicate. But I don't want that to distract us from this mission. My investigative deputy can call out the search for that body." The weapon finally drew his uncle's attention. "A CS5. A sniper rifle that can be pulled apart and stuck in a backpack."

"Perfect for hiking through the wilderness."

"And it'll take a .308, the bullet you found." His uncle held it up to the firelight for a closer look as he continued to speak in hushed tones.

"So you think it was our sniper?" Griffin asked.

"Could be. Could very well be. If so, he just spent hours hiking and climbing to get to us. Pretty determined."

"Maybe he knew he couldn't return without finishing his assignment." Nausea rolled through him at the thought.

His uncle only nodded, his gaze still on the weapon. "With this 12.5 short barrel, only law enforcement can legally carry it."

Griffin wanted to laugh. "What do criminals care about being legal? If they were worried about that, they wouldn't be illegally growing marijuana in the wilderness."

His uncle took the weapon parts over to his tent and stuck them inside, then returned to Griffin. "It's my turn to keep watch now. You get some rest."

Griffin was too tired to argue and knew he needed his strength for the morning that would come too early, so he turned and headed to the tent.

"Griffin, wait." His uncle's whisper was so low he almost hadn't heard it.

He returned to the fire and met his uncle's grave expression with his own.

"I understand that you feel something for Alice. That's all well and good, and I don't intend to stand in the way of what may come, but tomorrow, and for the next forty-eight to seventy-two hours, I need you on board. And we might as well get this straight here and now. If something goes wrong, I'm giving you the responsibility of getting that girl to safety. Don't worry about me or my deputies, we can take care of ourselves. Alice might think she's up for this, but you and I both know she isn't trained for what we might face. So something goes south you get Alice out. Her brothers would never forgive me if she got hurt. They might never forgive me as it is. Don't think of looking back or helping me. I need you to focus and not let your emotions get in the way—any obligation you might feel you have for me as your uncle or even any feelings you have for her. Am I clear? Her life, our lives might just depend on it."

Griffin took this one last opportunity, since his uncle had opened the door, to try to convince him to give this expedition up. "Are our lives worth it? Is the risk worth it? Let's head back tomorrow and give this up. For now."

"If we don't finish this... If we don't let Alice show us where and take us there so we can catch them, arrest the man after her, then she'll never stop looking over her shoulder. She could always have this guy hunting her. Is that what you want?"

Griffin stumbled to his tent. No. No, it wasn't what he wanted. Of course he didn't want this guy to be free to pursue and kill Alice. The thought made him nauseous. But when had what Griffin wanted ever made a difference?

Morning came much too early.

Alice had stayed up too late sitting by the fire with Griffin and after that she'd tossed and turned in her tent until she'd finally fell into an exhausted, fitful sleep. She'd dreamed some-one stalked them all the way to their camp on the river. She woke up in a cold sweat. The dream had felt so real that she climbed out of her sleeping bag and peeked through the zip-per of the tent, terrified of what she might see. But she only saw Sheriff Kruse walking the pe-rimeter, keeping watch. Though relief washed through her, she hadn't been able to fall back to sleep.

Not a great way to start what she expected to be one of the longest days of her life.

Everyone quickly ate and tore down their tents. Everyone except Deputy Edwards. His arm in a makeshift sling, his face appeared haggard and his moves were clumsy and slow, but that was to be expected after his injury. He looked miserable and probably couldn't wait for this to be over. She focused back on work-ing to secure the supplies in the raft. Fortu-nately, her patch remained secure and the raft well inflated.

Through it all, Alice made a point not to look at Griffin. At all. In her peripheral vision, she could see the guy putting away his precious camera. Maybe he'd been up before her taking a few snapshots. He had a bandage at his temple, too. When had that happened? Had he tripped and hit his head on a rock?

Needing an attitude check, she sucked in a deep breath.

If only she could just get last night out of her head. The feel of his touch against her cheek. The look in his eyes when he'd told her that she was beautiful. Even now warmth crawled over her at the memory, infusing her with an awareness she shouldn't have for him. He was much too appealing for Alice's good.

Why didn't you come back to Gideon?

Why, oh why, had she asked him that one last question? Why couldn't she just let it go? It had eaten her alive since his return. No, that was wrong. It had eaten her alive for the two years since he left. At first, she'd wondered when he'd come back, but then she'd finally realized and accepted he had no plans to return.

And now, here he was again. Of course, he hadn't come back to Gideon for *her* but to thrust himself in the middle of the combat action on this new battlefield. And Alice had just needed to ask him. Needed to hear the truth from him for herself instead of second-guessing the reasons.

And then his noncommittal reply of *I don't know*? Please. He didn't know why he hadn't come back to Gideon? What was that about? Was he a coward who couldn't tell her the truth? Or worse, a coward who couldn't admit the truth even to himself?

Dropping a box into the raft, her finger got caught. Pain shot through it. She jerked it back and shook out her hand. Wiped away the small issue of blood. At least her mistake and now the resulting throb yanked her back to reality. See? Thinking about Griffin like that was dangerous for them all, taking her attention from where it belonged—guiding them down the river and then leading them through the wilderness area.

Focus. Forget about him.

She was strong, physically strong, but when it came to Griffin, she was far too weak. No matter how she might have felt about him before, he wasn't someone she could ever trust. He had no staying power.

Everyone climbed into the raft as Alice released the rope that had secured it to the bank. Griffin sat in Alice's usual spot at the back and grabbed the main oars, then rowed them out into the smooth water. Alice held that position when it came to the rapids, but otherwise, she needed to use her strength efficiently. There were no rapids between this point and their destination, so she wasn't worried about someone else taking them for now. Later, she would be the one to take over again and maneuver them out of the middle of the river to the bank where they would exit the raft.

In the meantime, she tried not to watch Griffin. His strong hands gripping the oars. He'd removed the light jacket as the early morning chill lifted and now his biceps and broad shoulders working the oars could easily draw her attention. Unfortunately, she couldn't know if he was ignoring her, too, but he hadn't said one word to her this morning. Maybe they had both come to their senses and realized they needed to keep their distance.

Fine by her.

When they neared their place in the river where they would hike out to their final destination, Alice switched positions with Griffin and took the oars so she could steer the raft to the south bank. Across the way they spotted others breaking camp and readying for their day on the Rogue River. She wished she could join them and be a guide again with nothing worse to fear than a dunking courtesy of the rapids.

She hated that being forced back into the

Rogue had been the only way to get her back in the river, but now that she'd taken them through Blossom Bar and Picket Fence successfully, barring the gunshot incident, Alice's confidence had come back full force. Good thing, too. She needed that so she could see this through to the end.

At the small cove with a sandy beach on the south side, they tied off the raft and unloaded the supplies. Set up a small camp for Deputy Edwards. He couldn't keep up with them. He might as well stay with the raft and supplies and wait for their return. Starting on their journey from that point should take them a day at most to hike to the growing operation, perform reconnaissance and return.

Sheriff Kruse tried again to make his call on the SAT phone to whoever would coordinate the multi–task force effort, but couldn't get through. He was concerned, too, about contacting his department to let them know about the body that could be found downriver.

Alice was stunned by the news and demanded an explanation from the sheriff. He explained about Griffin's brush with a killer who'd found their camp. Her disturbed dream made sense now.

She fought the tears that threatened. She couldn't let Griffin see how weak she felt on the inside. Her dream, her terrible dream. Somehow her mind had known the battle that raged outside the tent and it had come into her dreams. Griffin's injury could have been so much worse. It served as a reminder of the possible dangers they faced going forward.

This atypical situation stretched his department, stretched them all—the sheriff, his accompanying deputies, Alice and Griffin—to their limits. She could see it in their eyes.

Feel it to her bones.

"Here you go." Sheriff Kruse held out a bulletproof vest—body armor for Alice.

"Are you asking me to wear that? It's too big and bulky." Not to mention it would restrict her movements and be entirely too hot. "I could get overheated."

"You're more of a target than we expected. Deputy Edwards is giving it up for you."

Right. Alice suspected Edwards couldn't wear the vest anyway with his injury.

The sheriff glanced at Griffin as though asking for his help in convincing Alice to wear the vest. What? Did he think that Griffin could talk her into it? Had he recognized her soft spot for his nephew? Of course. She'd been entirely too malleable when it came to Griffin. That much was apparently obvious to everyone.

She snatched the vest out of his hands. No

need for Griffin to get involved. He'd come along to take pictures and get a story. To be in the middle of the action. Fussing over her wasn't his responsibility. Sheriff Kruse was about to help her secure the vest but Griffin was the one to step up and assist. In fact, he grabbed it from Alice and pulled it apart to make sure the ballistic panels were inserted correctly. He gave his uncle a sheepish expression. "They could have shifted around after being packed away."

Sheriff Kruse didn't look convinced but shrugged, letting Griffin try to impress her with his knowledge or be the hero, she wasn't sure. When he appeared satisfied he lifted the vest over her, connected the fastenings on each side of her and adjusted the shoulder straps, repeatedly.

"It's important to make sure it doesn't sit too high or too low." He looked at the vest on her. "How's that? It should be about one inch below your diaphragm."

He glanced at her, waiting on her answer.

"I guess it is, I can't really tell."

"Lift your arms."

She did as he asked. He adjusted the sides. "Need to make sure they're equal on both sides."

"Why does it matter?"

"Because it will only protect what it covers."

When he finally appeared convinced that he'd positioned it correctly, he looked her up and down, giving her the distinct impression he wished he could cover her entire body with armor.

"I think it's too tight. I don't think I can breathe or move in this thing."

Sheriff Kruse looked to the sky and swiped his brow. "Hurry it up, already. This is taking too much time."

Griffin assisted her again in loosening the body armor but making sure it was still in the right position to protect her. His nearness, when she'd tried to avoid him all morning, was too much.

Too close, entirely too close. She shared a brief look with him. Way too much emotion boiled behind his gaze.

"Too bad you didn't bring a bulletproof helmet for her, too," he said, directing his words to his uncle. "Or better yet, let's call the whole thing off."

Alice had already stood her ground. Made her point last night. She wasn't turning back now. But putting on the vest drove home that she was in mortal danger.

Griffin handed off a bottle of water to her and apparently took that opportunity to lean in close. "I promised you I'd protect you. Stick close to me."

There wasn't any room in Griffin's heart for Alice. Not with his career taking center stage. Despite his promises, she couldn't let herself believe him, as much as she wanted to. And oh, how she wanted him to care about her that way. But she'd been burned by him before. She hardened her heart. "Don't give me that. You're not here for me. You have a story to get, re-member? That's why you're here. Don't try to make this about me."

"You're my priority now." He forced the words through gritted teeth. "Not the story. Don't you get it? You're more important."

Since when? "Why should I trust you? Huh?"

Who did this guy think he was? Besides being heartbreakingly charming with a rock-solid physique and killer smile? Alice wouldn't be fooled by any of that again. Especially in this situation where none of that mattered. Harder to dismiss was the way that Griffin was one of a kind—a guy with a big heart who single-handedly tried to take on all the evil in this world with his camera. That was something she couldn't so easily ignore.

Still, she brushed past him, her brutal words ricocheting back to her, raking over her—even though they'd been meant for him—and cutting her to the bone. Had the words hurt him, too? She wasn't sure if she should care, but it wasn't like her to be that cruel. She almost wanted to apologize for her outburst.

Though shaking, Alice closed her eyes, reining in her anger and calmed herself. There, now. No need to escalate things. She softened her next words. Evened out her tone. "I don't need your protection. I have a sheriff and deputy here. And now this trusty body armor to protect me."

They needed to work together as a team in this, but it was best he knew where she stood on the matter of his protection and her heart. She wouldn't let herself count on him.

Tugging the backpack over the body armor, and adding more than fifty pounds, she headed to the small creek that emptied into the Rogue, trusting the men would be right behind her.

"Let's get this over with."

"Hold up, Alice." The sheriff shifted into an authoritative posture that told her he would brook no argument. "You don't need to lead so much as guide. I want you in the middle so we can protect you in case we come across any hostiles. Let's hope we don't. Let's pray you can bring us close, and we'll reconnaissance and get out of Dodge before the men guarding the operation are the wiser. Once we top the rise overlooking the river, I'll try to use the SAT again and put in the call for the task force. The plan is that we'll have gathered and shared the information they'll need before they head out."

She nodded.

"After that," the sheriff continued, "no one talk. No one speak a word that could bring these guys down on us, warn them any more than they already are. That means we won't be scaring off the wildlife, either, and there's more than one kind of dangerous creature in the wilderness."

"You mean bears?" Griffin asked.

"And rattlesnakes."

And there they were, going right back into the viper's den.

With a pack strung across his back, his camera case positioned in front, weapons and ammo and gear racking up the pounds, the temperature in the high eighties, it was like being back in the Navy Combat Camera Unit again. He swatted at insects and reminded himself of the brutal heat in Iraq that could boil at over one hundred and twenty degrees, often feeling more like a hundred and sixty. Every region of the world had something harsh in its environment. He should be accustomed to this by now, and in a way he was, but it never got easier.

The heat and difficult terrain was to their disadvantage, forcing them to take far too many water breaks, which could put them seriously behind. Sitting on a boulder, he sipped water and rested. They'd all taken to the rocks to catch their breath. A few more miles and they would need to set up camp for the night if they didn't find the illegal garden by then. This landscape was too dangerous to travel after dark unless they had no other choice. They weren't going to make it in and out in one day like projected. Problem was, their camp might be entirely too close to the danger.

Griffin didn't like it. His uncle, the deputy and Alice weren't trained in military tactics. They didn't know how to evade discovery.

It didn't matter. They were there and discussing their plans was off the table for now. Couldn't make a sound to draw unfriendlies. Uncle Davis and Alice peered at a forest service map. She pointed but said nothing. Griffin hopped from his position and strode to them. He looked at the map, too. His uncle showed him their change in strategy. So apparently they could make changes in their plans, only silently.

They would take the long way around and come from the other side just to be safe in case they were expected from the north. It would take even longer, but at least they were going out of their way to make this as safe as possible. Griffin nodded his approval, as if he had any say in the matter, and eyed Alice as she drank more water. He read sheer exhaustion in her features.

This couldn't be over soon enough.

Watching and listening, they hiked quietly in a formation that allowed them to follow Alice's lead and protect her at the same time. A couple of hours later they came across another brook. Alice pointed south and nodded. This must be the one the men used to illegally divert water to their crops. She started hiking forward but his uncle grabbed her arm. He motioned for them to head west to the ridge a mile away. She must have forgotten their change of plans.

Once they reached the ridge, they dropped their packs. His uncle and Deputy Reed scouted the area and the rocky outcropping to make sure it was safe. Griffin stayed with Alice to protect her. Despite her words of bravado, she had to realize she was much safer with him, even if she would prefer he were someone else.

Why should I trust you? Huh?... I don't need your protection. I have a sheriff and deputy here. And now this trusty body armor to protect me.

This was the first moment Griffin had allowed himself to think about her words. Of course, he deserved them. He'd earned them fair and square. But the initial pain he'd experienced as she'd lashed out at him still made him wince at the memory. Since when had he let himself feel so much for one person that they could hurt him like that? He cared deeply for her, more than he truly wanted to admit, but he hadn't realized he'd let her get under his skin to that degree. If only his call-out to expose marijuana grown on public lands had brought him somewhere else, any place other than Alice's woods, then Griffin could have kept himself safe. Completely free of an entanglement with her. He thought he'd put enough distance between them, had enough fortification around his heart that he could safely go through this with her, but he had doubts, big fat doubts about that.

Griffin watched the woods before them, and the ridge behind them. The sun would drop behind the ridge to the west much too soon. He didn't like that they'd chosen to go that way. The ridge could be used to trap them, to ambush them, much like the cove where they had camped last night. The man who'd shot at them from the canyon on the river had climbed his way over and down into their camp last night. If Griffin hadn't sensed his presence... His breath hitched. Alice jerked her gaze to him.

He looked at her, saw in her expression the words she wouldn't speak. *What's wrong?* He changed his own demeanor to one of calm and shrugged, letting her know that he hadn't suddenly spotted imminent danger. But he could feel it crawling all over him, this time in the form of a thousand images from his past on countless battlefields. Those images burned in his mind as they had been on his camera. He closed the distance between them so he could be closer to her and protect her whether she liked it or not.

His uncle appeared around the rocks and Deputy Reed hiked from the other side, not nearly as quietly as he should. His uncle came close so he could whisper. "We're going to go in and get closer. Get the exact coordinates." He kept his voice low. Directing his next words specifically to Griffin, he said, "If you take a few pictures, that would help."

"And me?" Alice asked. "Just how close do you expect me to take you?"

"I want you to wait here until we get back. I don't want you in harm's way any more than necessary."

Griffin shook his head, kept his voice quiet. "I'm not going, then. I won't leave her alone. I'll climb up the ridge, get as high as I can. I see a terrace about halfway. From there I can grab pictures. The other images, the more detailed ones I came for, I can get when the task force rains down on this operation."

"Fair enough." His uncle nodded, appearing satisfied with Griffin's answer.

"No need for you to stay behind," Alice said. "I can protect myself. I've got my weapon. I'll stay hidden and quiet until you get back."

She really didn't want Griffin near her, did she? Well, he deserved all the venom she could send his way, he already admitted that.

"No, if he can get what he needs from the terrace, all the better. Griffin is staying. End of discussion."

His uncle motioned for Deputy Reed to join him and just before he turned to leave, Griffin grabbed his arm. "Be careful out there. They could have booby traps, too."

His uncle nodded and they disappeared in the woods.

Griffin closed his eyes and said a quick and silent prayer. *God, please protect them.* He feared for his uncle, his mom's brother, but the man was a sheriff and knew how to face danger head-on.

Griffin surveyed the ridge and once he spotted the best way to climb to the terrace, he started up. "You coming, or what?"

"No, I think I'll stay."

He paused and turned back to her. "We can get a better look at the operation from up there. We can see what's going on. I need to get those pictures and we need to stick together." Even better, they'd be at one of the highest points. Less risk that someone could sneak up on them. *I can keep you even safer.* "So why don't you grab your gun and some extra ammo, just in case." He hated thinking of the worst-case scenario, but had to be prepared.

Without another word Alice grabbed what she needed and beat him up and over the boulders to make the terrace. She sat back against a rock. He doubted she could see anything through the trees, but he positioned himself just right—flat against the boulder like a sniper—and looked through the lens of his camera, zoomed in.

His gut soured at what he saw.

The next thing he knew, Alice was next to him, flat against the boulder, too. "What is it? What do you see?" she whispered.

"It's not good. I don't think my uncle should have gone. Better to have done reconnaissance from here." Griffin could kick himself. He should have suggested that.

"How do we warn him?"

"We can't."

Griffin snapped a few pictures, taking in the

operation. His throat constricted. "Looks like thousands of plants."

He could make out over forty rows with maybe a hundred plants each, and that's only what he could see from there with an obstructed view. His pulse increased. Millions of dollars' worth of marijuana. Hadn't this been what he'd expected? What he'd wanted to document? The destruction to the wilderness—acres of felled trees, the pesticides, herbicides and fertilizers that harmed the wildlife and the waterways and fish. And the innocent people who stumbled on them like Alice. But dread settled in his gut at the massive number of guards. He could sense that something was about to go south, but he was stuck in this. Had to see it through.

"Can I look through it? See what you're seeing?"

She'd already seen some of it when she'd stumbled on it, but obviously not the vastness. "Sure, but you're not going to like it."

He handed over his superzoom camera, their fingers brushed, and his heart quickened.

"I don't see anything."

"From this distance you have to be right on it." He leaned in close and shifted the camera for her, catching the scent of her hair, mingled with river and pine needles and wilderness. *Alice...* If only he weren't damaged and flawed, he'd give anything to be the man for her. Griffin clamped down on those thoughts. Hadn't his uncle warned him to stay focused and not let his attention be distracted by his obvious feelings for this woman?

"Now can you see?"

She sucked in a breath.

Yeah, she saw it. That was all the answer he needed. "Did they have that many guards when you were there?"

"I mean, men chased me. Weapons fired off—I couldn't tell how many, just that there were a lot—but now it looks like…it looks like…"

"A war zone." Packed with armed guards ready to kill. A sickening feeling swelled in his stomach. This looked like a cartel operation. He should have expected as much, but he hadn't wanted to believe it.

Their little reconnaissance mission was a mistake. They shouldn't be there. Shouldn't have brought Alice. Griffin would need to search for an escape along the other side of this ridge. It surprised him there hadn't been a guard up on the ridge to begin with. Then a man's shadow fell over him and Alice. Griffin didn't miss the silhouette of the assault rifle.

EIGHT

They weren't alone.

Alice's heart palpitated. She sensed the moment Griffin had tensed. The instant he saw the shadow.

Milliseconds away from shooting them where they lay, the man quietly hovered over them with only his shadow giving him away. A scream lodged in her throat but couldn't escape. Fear paralyzed her. She couldn't move or make a sound. It was as though her mind believed if she stayed perfectly still she would be invisible to this killer.

What would Griffin do?

Before Alice could blink, he simultaneously shoved her away and twisted around, kicking the automatic weapon as it fired off multiple rounds into the air, all thanks to Griffin. He hopped to his feet and engaged the man in hand-to-hand combat, disarming him with frightening speed.

Griffin dodged the man's punches and landed his own into the man's nose, his throat and solar plexus, revealing he was much better trained at hand-to-hand combat than this man who obviously thought an automatic weapon could protect him.

Her Griffin could do that? She couldn't believe her eyes. She'd always just thought of him as a photographer. A journalist. But he'd been a combat photographer trained for combat in all branches of the military, like he'd told her repeatedly. Why was she surprised?

Curses spewed from the man he'd disabled.

Groaning, he lay in agony on the ground, gripping his broken arm. He was no longer a threat to them. But by firing off his weapon, he'd alerted the others that they were there. Automatic weapon fire resounded somewhere in the distance through the woods. Had their reconnaissance team—the sheriff and his deputy—been discovered, too? Or had the weapon fire been in response to the man Griffin had disarmed?

Shouts rang out.

Oh, Lord, please help them! Help us! She couldn't go through this nightmare again. She'd been through it before with Marie. She gasped for breath. All she wanted to do was crumple and curl into a ball and hope it would all just go away.

"What should we do? Where should we go?" she asked.

Snatching up his camera—which he'd apparently protected like he'd protected Alice—Griffin gripped her arm. "Away. We're getting out of here now."

He tugged her in the direction from which the man had come—toward the highest point of the ridge, instead of returning where they'd climbed up. She glanced back at the man writhing in pain. She still couldn't get over how fast Griffin had acted. How completely competent and fierce he'd been, breaking a few of the man's bones, rendering him harmless.

At the ridge he glanced up, clearly looking for a way to climb it.

"Why are we going this way?" she asked. "The sheriff will be coming for us. What if he needs us?"

"My uncle will have to find his own way. He charged me to protect you if anything went wrong. To get you back to safety. He trusts me to protect you, Alice, now if only you would do the same."

She had refused to let him know she accepted him as her protector, but she'd wanted him there with her, though she hadn't wanted to admit that even to herself. And that was before she'd seen him in action. She would trust him to protect her now against these guys, but that was as far as her trust went.

"But your uncle and Deputy Reed, they could need our help."

"Like I told you, my uncle and I have already discussed this. Any trouble goes down, then my job is to get you out of here."

"Oh yeah? Where was I when these decisions were made without my input? Why bring me at all?"

"Would you agree that there's no time to argue?" His slate-gray eyes pinned her.

With rapid gunfire rattling in the woods all around them, shaking her heart up in her chest, Griffin had a point. "Yeah, sure, we can talk later," she said.

"Good. Now, I'm assuming you can climb. It's more difficult than the terrace we made."

"I know how to climb, but I'm rusty."

"Rusty will have to do." Griffin started up. "Besides, even a novice could scale this."

"What about him?" She gestured to the man who'd almost killed them. "Are we going to just leave him? Should we arrest him or something?"

"Not this time." Griffin stared at the rock wall, presumably planning his route. They didn't have climbing gear or ropes so there would be no room for mistakes.

He took off quickly and she watched his path. Drew in a few deep breaths that weren't as calming as she'd hoped. Her backpack in place, she followed him up, concentrating on the best place to grip the rocks with her bare hands and booted feet.

"You can do this," Griffin said. He must have sensed her anxiety, or he had a healthy dose of his own fear. "You can do this and you can survive. Don't think about anything else."

Right, because if she couldn't climb this wall, she wouldn't survive.

In this moment, that was all that mattered. The gunfire behind her didn't matter. The sheriff and Reed were on their own. If Alice didn't get a good grip on her climb she'd fall and break something important or hit her head and die. She tried to push aside the terror coming at her from all sides.

Taking deep breaths, she forced out a few words, hoping Griffin's answer would settle at least some of the fear. "Do you think they'll see us?"

"Not unless they're looking."

Which they very well could be considering the gunfire from their would-be killer. As if he'd heard their conversation from several feet below them, he shouted out to notify his buddies in crime that Alice and Griffin were getting away.

"Or that guy draws attention to us," Griffin added.

Halfway up the ridge. "Should we go back and knock him out or something?"

"Not a bad idea." Griffin started down. "You keep going. I'll meet you at the top."

"Wait. I didn't mean it. I was only kidding."

"Go!"

Why couldn't she just keep her mouth shut? She focused on the ridge and the path Griffin had been following, the slight creases, subtle edges in the granite, the small protrusions she could grip with her fingers.

Sweat poured from her body, drenching her and making her hands slicker than was safe. She could lose her grip.

Oh, God, please protect us. Please help us to get away from these men. Help the sheriff and Deputy Reed find their way to safety, too. Blind the bad guys to our presence or hold them back. Something, God, I'm begging You. But in all of this bring justice to this outrage in the forest!

Praying helped ease her fear and kept her focused. Before she realized it, she was almost to the top. But what of Griffin? She glanced down just as he hit the man in the head with his own weapon, and then Griffin thrust the guy's automatic weapon over his own shoulder before starting up the ridge again. Alice continued her climb and made the top, crawling over and onto the flat surface, but she pressed her body down against the granite so no one would be able to take a shot at her like what happened on the river. Now that she'd made the ridge, she willed her heart rate and breathing to slow, counting on the fact Griffin wouldn't be long in joining her.

A few minutes later, his hands finally gripped the edge and he pulled himself up and crawled over, meeting her at the top. He eyed her, sweat beading on his brow and dripping into his gray eyes. He gasped for breath and pressed his forehead against the rock. He growled through his gulps for air. "I'm getting out of shape."

"It's my fault. I shouldn't have suggested we silence the guy down there. You wouldn't have had to crawl back down and then up again."

Automatic weapon fire continued in the woods but it sounded farther away this time as if the men were heading in the opposite direction. Were they going after the sheriff and deputy? Her insides twisted up in knots she might never unravel. "I'm worried about them. Isn't there anything we can do to help?"

"The plan is that I get you out of here, and go around if possible. We'll meet back at the raft and take it the rest of the way. If my uncle has caught their attention, then he'll be leading them away from us and that's what it sounds like is happening. What we don't know is how far these men will follow them. How far did you have to run before they stopped chasing you?"

"I don't know. I think the gunfire ended long before I ever stopped running. I think that's because of the guy who recognized me..." Her throat seized up again. "Because..." Oh, why couldn't she say the words?

His hard gaze turned soft. "Why waste bullets if he knows where to find you. Is that what you wanted to say?"

"Yeah. That."

He shook his head. "Except for the fact now you're showing us where his operation is. No, I believe he wanted to stop you, but you lost them in the woods, Alice. That's all there is to it. And unfortunately, yeah, he did know where to find you." Griffin's gaze turned dark and cloudy. What was he thinking? "Okay, well, you ready? We need to get moving. We don't want another one of the men to come up behind us. Are you up for covering a lot of ground?"

She nodded. "Always. Especially if crazy people with automatic weapons are chasing me."

Griffin had come close to telling her what he'd been thinking. Was it possible the guy wanted her alive? That keeping her alive was important to him? But Griffin hadn't wanted to scare Alice. He needed her to focus on getting back to safety, just as he had to focus.

At the top of the ridge, they crept low as they moved to the opposite end. The sun shone hot and bright from the west as it made its descent. It would set much too soon, making their trek far more difficult. An eagle screeched above them. A sound that would normally draw his attention skyward so he could take a moment to enjoy the sight. But not in this moment when they were literally fleeing for their lives. Not in this moment when every second counted. If they could escape unscathed, thanks to his uncle, all the better. Still, he sent up continuous prayers for his uncle and Deputy Reed.

On the other side they found a short edge that fell away into a steep, tree-covered slope. Beyond that, a deep canyon trapped them. Griffin hopped down, felt his boots on the ground. Glanced up in time to see Alice jump from the wall next to him. The heavy pack knocked her off balance so she plopped on her backside.

He offered his hand. She hesitated before taking it and he helped her to her feet.

"So what now?" she asked.

"Can you lead us back to the raft? My uncle should be heading that way, too, as soon as he can, and maybe we'll meet back up on the path at some point."

"Griffin." The way she said his name jerked his gaze back from the wilderness around them. "What if we don't run into him on the way back or at the raft? What then?"

Griffin hadn't wanted to think about that possibility. "We'll figure that out then, if it comes to that."

She scowled at him before starting off. "You guys should have let me in on this part of the plan where you turn bodyguard. I would have picked a different escape path. Now we have a lot of hiking ahead of us to make it back to the raft."

"I didn't pick the ridge, you did. It is what it is." Now deal with it. *But you're safe, Alice, at least for the moment.* That's all that mattered to Griffin. But he hated his harsh tone.

"Like we had a lot of choices."

"Look, you guided us here to this operation, but you don't need to be in the combat zone. And I'm glad I stayed behind to protect you."

"But I kept you from being in the middle of

the action. That's what you wanted, isn't it? It's why you're here. The whole reason you came back to Gideon." Alice stopped and turned to face him.

"Sure, yeah. I won't lie about that. But how many times do I have to tell you that you're more important? You're my priority." He wished Alice hadn't had to guide them to begin with. He never imagined it would come to this. And now they were fighting over it.

"The way you protect your camera while you fought that guy, you have a couple of priorities." She glanced at his camera.

Sure he'd protected his camera. Why shouldn't he? "What would you have done up against that guy and his AR-15 assault rifle, huh?"

The hostility in her gaze melted away. Admiration took its place. "The way you fought him was amazing. I never knew…"

"What? That I had skills?" He exhaled. Scraped a hand through his hair. "How do you think I survived in the middle of war zones?"

Concern etched her features. For him? She shrugged. "How much do you think all those plants are worth, anyway?"

He welcomed the subject change. "I couldn't say exactly. But my estimate based on the plants I could see is no less than fifteen million dollars. That's why those men are still there, even after they knew they'd been discovered. They know it won't be easy for law enforcement to take them down. They have ample firepower and excellent reasons to put up a fight instead of surrendering quietly or choosing to cut and run."

Her exhausted features visibly paled. "I guess we'd better get going."

She hiked down the slope, leaning into the hill, sliding some of the time, pressing hard and fast. Griffin kept up with her. They couldn't keep this pace up for too long, but best to put as much distance as they could between them and anyone who might be pursuing them. He shared Alice's concern for his uncle and Deputy Reed. And a measure of guilt for not running into the fray to assist, but his mission parameters had been clear. His only goal was to get Alice back to safety.

The sound of automatic gunfire still rattled faintly in the distance to the east of them. There was no doubt they would be outgunned if facing an all-out gun battle. Images—those he'd caught on camera in his many past assignments—flashed through his mind. Hundreds of horrific images. As always, pain came with them. Unfortunately for him, he'd never grown callous no matter how much he'd seen.

"Griffin." Alice shook him.

He opened his eyes. She stared at him, her dark blue eyes troubled. "What's wrong? Why are you just standing there with your eyes closed? You look like you're in pain."

He hadn't realized when he'd stopped following her. "Sorry, I just needed a second to catch my breath."

Her furrowed brows softened. "Okay. Maybe we should take a break. Hydrate." She plopped on a flat rock and grabbed her water.

Griffin joined her on the rock and poured cold water on his hot head.

"That's a great idea." She followed suit, then turned to him, blinking away the water with her long eyelashes.

"Feeling better?"

"All better, yes." Though tenuous, her smile was still beautiful. Maybe even contagious.

He loved the nature-girl look and her self-confidence. She never acted concerned about her appearance, and why should she? She was beautiful, both on the outside and the inside. Strong and vibrant. She was everything he could ever want and need, that is, if he allowed himself that luxury.

Her smile quickly faded. "What happened back there?"

"What, you mean just now?"

"Yeah, when you stopped. Are you sure you're not hurt? That guy you fought didn't wound you somewhere, did he?"

"No, nothing like that." He hung his head. Shook it. Pushed away the images. "It's just that I've taken a lot of pictures of horrific things over the years. Seen things I can't un-see, you know?" He glanced at her. Gauged her reaction.

She nodded, but he was certain she didn't actually know. How could she? He was glad she didn't. He'd shield her from all the ugliness in the world if he could.

"Sometimes those images come back to me at the worst times and—" he pressed his fist against his chest "—the pain gets me right here every time."

Birdsong filled the trees around them. A chipmunk skittered past. Nature appeared undisturbed here as though nothing foul poisoned the environment a few miles away.

"I'm sorry, Griffin. I didn't realize it all affected you so much. I wish there was something I could do for you to erase all that." She hesitated, clearly debating with herself whether to continue, then added, "But it seems to me that you keep running back to it."

He nodded. How did he explain to her something he didn't understand himself? Was he some sort of addict? Addicted to capturing the worst possible scenes? Hooked on the adrenaline or the action? No. Deep down, that wasn't it at all. "I don't know, Alice. If I could change who I am, I would. But I'm compelled to shine the light in the darkness. To expose the evil that happens all around us, sometimes too close to home, like in this situation. But I'm compelled to somehow help to make things right. Does that make sense to you?"

Again he saw the admiration in her dark blue eyes. It was as if she tried to see right into his soul. Griffin looked away. He couldn't hold her beautiful gaze too long, especially opening up like this, letting her see him…exposed. And yet, there was nothing he wanted more. What was it about her that made him want to curl her up into his arms and hold her forever?

"It makes sense. It's what I admire about you."

Griffin frowned. He couldn't let her get too close. Best to do as his uncle said and focus on getting her to safety. "You and me running from what's practically a small army— I never imagined this scenario. I feel like I'm getting too close to the battlefield again, and with someone I—" *care deeply about.* He'd said far too much. Didn't dare look at her.

A sound disturbed him, or rather the lack of sound. Everything had grown quiet. No more birdsong. Griffin locked gazes with Alice and held a finger to his lips, then motioned for her to stay where she was. He lifted the automatic weapon he'd snatched from the guy on the ridge and crept through the trees in the direction from which they'd come. He peered through the lens of his camera and used it like a pair of binoculars.

His spirits sank at what he saw.

Three armed men clambered down the side of the ridge.

They were being hunted.

NINE

Alice was so thirsty, she wanted to drink more but she knew it was smarter to conserve resources when she had no idea what they would face. If they would have time to stop and gather more water to filter. But she grew impatient waiting on Griffin. Impatient and worried.

He'd disappeared through the dense trees minutes ago.

Alice kept still and listened, growing more anxious by the second. She put her water away and palmed her weapon. Might as well prepare for the worst.

Had he heard something more than the complete silence around them that had spooked him? Though she imagined the sudden silence would be enough to put him on alert, and send him away to scout out danger. She didn't blame him for going to check things out, she just hated being left behind. But he was better trained in conflict. If she kept to what she did best—

guiding and wilderness survival—and let him rely on his experience and training, then they'd both be better off.

Alice needed his protection. She wanted it, so why couldn't she just admit that to him, and show him that she appreciated his efforts on her behalf? But she knew why. She just didn't want to be beholden to him in any way.

Twigs snapped and leaves rustled.

Gripping her gun, Alice slowly stood and moved behind a tree trunk. She held the weapon up, aimed it into the woods in the direction from which the sounds had come, as she watched and waited.

Please, God, please let Griffin be the next person I see. Or at least someone with our group.

Her prayer was answered as Griffin emerged, rushing out of the greenery, wide eyes determined. "Run!"

He caught her wrist as he passed her, barely slowing down, and tugged her behind him. She stumbled at first but quickly got the message and kept up. His action reminded her of when she'd done the same to Marie on her mad dash from the bad guys. Only this time she still had her pack.

Alice didn't bother asking him what was

going on. She knew. They were being followed. Hunted.

She pushed ahead. "Let me lead," she forced through her panicked breaths.

She focused on one thing only. Taking the most direct path out of this wilderness nightmare. She paused long enough to drop her pack, knowing the weight would only slow them down. Griffin did the same. They tossed the packs to the west to lead the men away as they headed north and east. Was she a wilderness survivalist or not? She could get them through without the packs.

Right now they needed speed.

Running through the underbrush, hopping over fallen logs and jumping boulders like an athlete in an Olympic hurdling event, she listened for Griffin's heavy gasps and footfalls behind her, but had no doubt he could keep up. As the minutes went by their pace slowed. There was no way to keep running through the rough terrain at full throttle. Alice paused behind a tree to catch her breath.

Griffin bumped into her, then caught her up, grabbed her like he thought he would knock her over. Not so easy to do. Lean muscle made up Alice's frame.

She gasped for breath. "How. Far. Behind. Are they?" she asked.

Bent over his thighs he shook his head. "I don't know. I doubt they were able to match our pace, but they're probably still following our tracks. If providence is on our side they might even get lost while searching."

Griffin leaned against the tree trunk. Closed his eyes. He still had his weapons, and the automatic weapon slung over his shoulder. He lowered it to the ground, his hand hovering over it so that he could grab it again in a hurry.

"We need to keep moving." His features were pinched.

She nodded. "What happens if they catch up?" What a dumb question. But maybe she asked it so that Griffin would feed her some small encouragement.

Opening his eyes, he stared into the woods, something feral and terrifying in his gaze. "You'd better pray that doesn't happen."

They were safe for the moment, but the look in his eyes and his tone had terror squeezing her insides. Could anything be worse than what she'd already gone through? Yes. Yes, it could. She swallowed and allowed determination to fill her. They could do this. They could beat these men that had no right to destroy the wilderness, no right to chase them and try to kill them. Alice would focus on surviving so that she could take them down once and for all. And so she wouldn't have to be afraid they would track her down one day and kill her.

"Okay, then. Are we still heading back to the raft?" she asked. "Because that could put us in harm's way, too."

"Unless you want to contend with that canyon, I don't see another choice but to head that way."

Alice grew antsy as they caught their breath, picturing all the ways this could go wrong. "What if we holed up somewhere and hid until the task force gets here?"

He pushed from the trees and gathered the automatic weapon into his arms like he would use it. "I'm thinking that's a worst-case scenario. But at least it's on the table."

Then he surprised her with a grin and a wink. "Good thing for me I'm in this with a wilderness survival guide."

His words warmed her insides. "Don't kid me. You were in the military. You've got survival skills, too."

"True, but this is your home field we're playing in. You have the advantage." He eyed the woods behind them, then lowered his voice. "Now, lead on. We shouldn't take any more breaks for a while."

Alice agreed. She picked up her pace again and hoped no one in the group of men after them had any tracking experience. Since their main obligation was to guard the illegal marijuana growing operation, there was no reason why tracking should be among their skills, but one never knew. It wasn't like she and Griffin had gone out of their way to hide their tracks, but when they came across a creek she saw it as their chance to do just that.

She followed the brook, stepping in the water up to their ankles—low this time of year—maneuvering across slippery boulders. They would need to stop and hydrate soon. She might consider using water from this brook but it could be contaminated with chemicals from the marijuana farm. Chemicals that even her water filtration might not be able to remove, had she not tossed her pack. They could wait to drink later, but she paused for a moment to catch her breath.

Gunfire resounded in the near distance. Multiple rounds.

Her knees shook.

She jerked her gaze to Griffin. "What are the chances your uncle and the deputy made it out okay?"

"That gunfire could mean they're still looking for them. The men after us are coming more from the west." He eyed the water, thirst in his gaze and licked his lips. Then he looked at her.

She shook her head. "Too risky this close to the farm. We need to wait." Without the filtration, drinking any water was a big risk, even without the issue of chemicals from the illegal growing operation.

"How much farther before we reach the base camp and Edwards?"

"What if they discovered the camp already? Remember that someone shot at us on the river. Tried to harm us at last night's camp, too."

"He could have radioed about our location, but I think his job was to stop us and I killed him before he got the chance."

Griffin gripped the rifle and stared into the woods.

Had he heard their pursuers getting closer? He gestured toward the brook and their path. "How much farther?" he asked again.

"A half a day."

Griffin stiffened.

"I'm… I'm sorry. But we put a lot of distance between us and the Rogue River when we took the long way around and then added more going over the other side of that ridge."

His expression turned grim.

An armed man stepped from the trees and aimed his weapon at them.

Though caught by surprise, instinct kicked in. In less time than it took to blink, Griffin's mind processed his best chance of success—wait to be captured or gunned down? Or shield Alice, protect her life at any cost?

Griffin shoved her behind the tree as pain sliced across his side and bullets ripped past him.

"Griffin! You're shot!" Her words sounded distant.

He pressed her down behind the tree and returned fire. Heart pounding, adrenaline pumping, he prayed as bullets spilled from the AR-15 he'd taken. Alice pressed her hands over her ears and Griffin wished he could do the same, the terrible *rat-a-tat* of the deadly weapon accosting not only Griffin's eardrums but also his soul with horrifying mental images of bodies falling.

God, please, I don't want to do this! I don't want to have to use this weapon. I don't want to hear the sound. I don't want to kill anyone but I have no choice. Let only one guy be here. Please let me take him out of commission. Help me to protect her.

Breathing hard, he pressed his back against the trunk again. Griffin listened for the man, or more men, while he frantically searched the wilderness in front of him for an out. Did he tell her to run this time? Or would that mean her death? He wasn't thinking clearly, wasn't analyzing quickly enough. What was wrong with him?

Get Alice to safety. That was all that mattered.

He caught his breath and let his heart rate slow. When the answer came to him, his gut tied into knots. He had no real options. They wouldn't be running this time. He'd have to face the man head-on. Take him out before he and Alice could push toward their base camp on the Rogue River. This experience sent his mind back to the bloodshed. Gunfire. Rocket launchers. IEDs—improvised explosive devices.

Now they were in the war zone together, something he never could have imagined or wanted for Alice. Surviving under these circumstances seemed impossible, like the most extreme sport that tempted fate.

Only God could help them.

Griffin hoped that God would answer his prayers.

He flicked his gaze to his right where Alice remained silent, terror in her eyes. He caught her watching him, waiting anxiously for his suggestion. She wouldn't like it. And frankly neither did he. Would he ever see her again? A knot lodged in his throat. He swallowed.

"Run for your life," he whispered, or at least

he hoped he'd whispered. Hard to tell with his ears still ringing from the AR-15 modified to fully automatic. "I'll find you, or I'll meet you at the Rogue River. Just run until you're safe."

"But…"

He didn't give her a chance to argue. Sucking in a breath, he marched around the tree and pressed his finger against the trigger guard, holding it there to release a stream of bullets into the woods as he continued forward, hating the damage to the trees and potentially the wildlife but prioritizing Alice's life which was on the line. His life, too. His tactic was part intimidation and part desperation.

Behind the protective barrier of a tree trunk, Griffin saw the man who'd come for them. His dark eyes grew wide when he caught Griffin's fearless approach. His determined hike had clearly had the intended effect. Still, the man lifted his weapon. Griffin aimed his sidearm, this time, point-blank at the man's face. "Put your weapon down or I swear, I'll kill you where you stand."

Oddly, the man simply grinned.

Pain sliced Griffin's head as something clubbed him from behind. Darkness edged his vision but he fired his weapon, then focused and swung around. A fist slammed into his face. He ignored the pain—their lives were on the line—and fought back. He had to buy Alice time to get away. A big, dirty man slammed him into the tree. Too dazed to recover, he slid to the ground. He tried again to lift his arms, but they hung at his sides. He couldn't stand. Couldn't fight.

Couldn't save Alice.

God, please let her get far enough away. Get to safety.

Maybe it had never been his responsibility to begin with. His compulsion to make a better world suddenly meant nothing to him if the one woman he cared about came to harm. His only hope was in God.

God, help us! Save Alice!

A man pressed his face in toward Griffin's. Spewed words Griffin heard but didn't really take in, his hot breath and spittle hitting Griffin. He squeezed his eyes shut. He'd failed. *Oh, God, I failed!* Anger surged. His limbs became responsive again, but it was too late, they were still not quick enough. He couldn't move fast enough to disarm this guy.

The man stood and aimed his weapon at Griffin. Was that it, then? Would he die like this?

A woman screamed. *Alice!*

"No!" She stepped in front of Griffin.

"What are you doing?" He ground out the

words. "Get out of here. You should have run. Don't save me!"

"No," she whimpered, her tone begging. "Please, don't kill him."

Was she putting on some kind of act? That didn't sound like the Alice he knew. She would never beg... Except for that one time when she'd begged him not to leave her behind... but... Griffin tried to push to his feet. He received a kick and a punch. A throbbing sensation was all he could feel through the numbness.

Alice screamed again. It ripped through him, clawing at him.

He tried to call out, but nothing but groans escaped.

He rolled to his side. Through the trees he witnessed a man pulling Alice by her ponytail. Anger seared through him. He got to his knees. Said a quick, silent prayer. Searched for his weapons. Nothing. The men had disarmed him. Why hadn't they killed him? Maybe they thought they'd left him for dead. They weren't wrong. In this wilderness and in this heat, he'd never make it out alive, at least on his own.

Their mistake? Leaving him to draw another breath. And then another. He would not let them take Alice. That alone fueled him with fury that coursed through his veins and ramped up a fresh new surge of adrenaline. He stood, let the dizziness pass, then quietly followed them. He was in stealth mode on the battlefield again to get the picture. Only this time it wasn't about capturing images, it was about saving the girl. His Alice. Maybe he could never truly be with Alice, but he thought of her as his now.

He had one mission and one goal. To take those men down before they harmed her. Images of what they could do to her flashed across his vision, but he shook them off. They were too horrifying and dwelling on them would debilitate him.

Alice fought the man who dragged her. Kicked him in the groin. The other man—the one he had threatened to kill but obviously missed when he'd fired his weapon—shoved her down and pointed his weapon at her, pressing the muzzle into her cheek and moving it around.

Then a wicked grin slid onto his face. "I think we should have some fun with you before we deliver you. That would teach you a lesson."

Alice spit in his face. "I'm not going to give you the chance."

Good girl. She had no intention of backing down or letting these men see the fear she must feel deep inside. And Griffin had no intention of letting them work her over until they saw her fear.

It was now or never.

He burst through the thick undergrowth, surprising them as he tackled the man holding Alice. Griffin grabbed the man's weapon and fired it, taking out the bigger man. He killed him.

Then he focused on the man who'd released Alice. Griffin slammed the butt of the firearm into the man's head, giving as good as he got. He pointed the weapon, pressing the barrel into the man's cheek just as he'd seen him do to Alice.

"You. Will. Not. Touch her. Again." More venom filled his words than he'd ever experienced. He tried to catch his breath, but his mind still burned with one, all-encompassing thought.

Not Alice. They wouldn't touch her, take her from him. His heart hammered as fury exploded. He wanted to hurt this man, watch him writhe in pain and then kill him.

She grabbed his arm and shouted. "He's unconscious!" Her words barely filtered through his rage.

"Griffin." She gripped his shoulders and spoke softly this time. "Griffin…what are you doing? He can't hurt us. They can't hurt us anymore. Let's go, let's get out of here."

He blew out a breath and hit the man again

for good measure. What was the matter with him? All the violence he'd seen, the atrocities, and he didn't want to be part of that. He hated inflicting violence. And now, he was no better than these men.

"Griffin, look at me." Alice pressed her hands against his cheeks and turned him to face her.

He looked into her blue eyes, saw the storm raging there.

"Breathe, just breathe," she said.

He nodded. He should be comforting her. But there was no time. Pressing his hand over hers on his cheek, he gripped it, and together they ran, not taking time to process what had just happened. They didn't have the luxury. It would have to wait until much later. Right now they had to give escaping their all. Except hadn't they done that already? Ran as hard and as fast as they could. Done everything within their power to lose these men? And yet it hadn't been good enough.

This ordeal had tested his stamina, his mental acuity and self-control like nothing else he'd experienced. For the first time in his life doubt infused his soul that he was strong enough to get out of this alive, and he struggled to hold on to hope. He struggled to hide that from Alice.

They found the brook again and she stepped

into the water, Griffin following, and led them north, always north toward the Rogue River. They stayed in the brook to minimize their tracks, continuing their exhausting trudge for a mile before crossing the brook. The sound of the clear water flowing over rocks ignited his thirst. He wanted to drop his face in the cool stream. But they couldn't stop. Could never stop until she was safe.

Except she did finally slow, her legs visibly trembling in front of him as she gasped for breath.

"Alice?"

Suddenly she crumpled against a tree. Fell to her knees.

And Griffin knew now was that moment when they would come to terms with what had happened back there. He dropped beside her. Gathered her into his arms. He thought she might sob into his shoulder, but she didn't. Instead she shook. His insides shuddered with her. He held her close, wanting to protect her from all the evil in this world—and he'd seen too much already. He squeezed his eyes shut against the atrocities, the images flashing in his mind, and tried to shove away the one image that would undo him—what could have happened to her had Griffin been killed. What could have happened to her if the men had succeeded in taking her back to their criminal operation.

He couldn't think about it.

Brushing his hand down her soft hair, knowing her head likely hurt from being pulled by her ponytail, he held her until they both calmed down. Maybe they could remain hidden for a while and no one would come after them.

Alice sighed, long and heavy.

She eased away from him, her expressive eyes caressing his face and pooling with tears. She brushed a finger over his face and he winced. "You're hurt. They beat you. You... could have died."

I would have died a thousand times over if they'd taken you from me. "I don't care. I only care that you're okay, but you're not safe yet. We can't rest for long, we have to get out of here."

A single tear slid down her dirty cheek, cutting a clean line through the grime. Griffin wanted to cry with her. And he wanted so much more than he could ever ask from her. Closing his eyes, he leaned in and pressed his lips against hers, drinking in all that was Alice. Her soft lips tender against his, she didn't pull away. Emotion poured from her, the want, the need to fulfill their connection. This wasn't the time or the place for a kiss, no matter how innocent, but after facing death, after coming so close to losing their lives, he'd take this one thing for himself. This one selfish act.

And kiss Alice. Because he didn't have the luxury of loving her.

A few yards away leaves rustled, footfalls accompanied grunts.

Oh, God, please...not again. Griffin never thought it would come to this, but he began to question their chances of survival.

TEN

Alice reached for her weapon. Needed to feel her hand around the grip. Heart hammering, she knew she wouldn't let them hurt Griffin or take her. No way would she go with them again. Though terrified, she vowed to die rather than go with these men if it came to that.

But her holster…it was empty. Oh yeah. In their rush to get away, she hadn't searched for the weapon they'd taken. She'd been stripped of that. Nearly stripped of her dignity, too, if it hadn't been for Griffin. *If he hadn't shown up to help*… She couldn't think about what might have happened back there because she faced a new threat now.

And panic set in, her pulse ratcheting up. How would they defend themselves if they couldn't escape these monsters? At least Griffin had grabbed the monsters' weapons. He'd been thinking straight—well, besides that moment when he almost beat that man to death.

He'd taken their weapons so they couldn't be used against them again, and so he could protect himself and Alice.

She'd only *imagined* herself strong and capable. She'd been anything but strong back there.

Thank You, God, thank You...for sending Griffin. For saving him, and helping him to save me.

But now they had to face a new threat, and her nerves teetered on the edge of complete collapse. She knew everything about how to survive in the wilderness, and only a little about battling evil men with automatic weapons intent on killing.

When Griffin stood, holding the automatic weapon he'd taken from the man he'd killed, she hunkered behind him, stunned that she'd instinctively used him as her protective barrier. Something she never would have done before this experience.

He stiffened and raised the weapon. "Run, Alice! Run and hide. Don't forget what happened last time when you didn't heed my warning."

Oh, she hadn't forgotten. Could never forget. Everything in her wanted to run, but she wouldn't leave him behind to die for her. They were in this together.

Griffin positioned the weapon and tensed.

He would spray the woods with bullets again, killing the men before they even had a chance to attack them.

"Don't shoot!" A familiar voice reached her through the underbrush.

In the distance, Sheriff Kruse emerged from the trees, holding up a blood-splattered, wounded deputy who he half dragged toward them. The sight startled and horrified her at the same time. Griffin also appeared stunned and slowly lowered the weapon. He rushed forward, Alice right behind him, and reached his uncle. Assisted him with Deputy Reed.

A strange mixture of utter dread and relief surged through her. The two men had survived and found them on their trek back to the Rogue, but her heart tumbled at the sight of Deputy Reed's condition. She was afraid to ask questions. Afraid of the answers. She sensed they all needed to remain positive. They needed to believe it was possible to live through this ordeal. They needed hope so they could endure. Talking about Deputy Reed's condition could strip them of that.

Griffin took the deputy from his uncle and supported his weight, looking like he was about to lower him to the ground.

"No time to stop. Let's keep moving." Sheriff Kruse swiped sweat from his eyes with his forearm. "Let's get *much* farther away and then we can use the emergency kit in your packs to see to his wound—we left our backpacks behind—but we can't stay here to do that. Too dangerous."

Alice and Griffin shared a glance. He shook his head. "We did the same, trying to make a getaway."

Furrows creased the sheriff's brow, but he nodded. "Let's keep going, then. The sooner we get out of here, the better."

"I'll assist Deputy Reed, then," Griffin said.

The man grunted as Griffin shifted his position.

Sheriff Kruse nodded his agreement. "I wasn't sure how much longer we could keep going. Glad we found you when we did. Just in time."

"I'll help, too," Alice said.

"You can try when I get tired, but he might be too heavy. You just lead us out of here."

Alice pushed ahead of them and led them farther down to another brook which they could follow out since it flowed toward and emptied into the Rogue River.

"How did you find us?" she asked.

"Find you? I thought you were waiting for us," Sheriff Kruse said. "We were looking for the brook that could lead us toward the Rogue River."

That made sense. If she wasn't still shaken, she might have realized it sooner. Alice nodded as she focused on her path in the brook, waters sloshing as they kept moving, hiking right in the water to hide their tracks.

"But I saw Griffin holding that weapon," the sheriff continued. "Got a glimpse of that through the trees and was afraid he was about to gun us down. That's why I called out to you. I didn't want to give us away because we've been retreating since almost the first moment we got close to the garden. But I've had my fill of being shot at, and didn't much like the idea of taking a bullet from friendly fire."

Alice glanced behind them. Griffin struggled with Deputy Reed. Concern they wouldn't make it stalked her. She started back to help Griffin.

Sheriff Kruse caught her arm. "He's fine, Alice. You just lead us out of here as fast as you can. I've called for backup. Called in the law to rain down on these ravening insects eating up our forest. Stay focused on getting us out."

"I thought you'd already done that."

"I let them know to get started on assembling. Problem is that takes a lot of time. And I had to investigate the site to know what was required, especially when multiple agencies are involved. You understand that, right?"

"Sure. I guess. But how long will that take them?"

He frowned. "Unfortunately I don't know for certain. And considering the firepower we're up against, we're calling in reinforcements from other agencies which could take longer than I'd like. It's a good thing we took a look first so we knew what to ask for, though we haven't come away unscathed." The sheriff caught his breath. "But there's no way we can wait on them to get these men off our tail. It'll take too long. We're on our own, so let's keep moving."

Before the sheriff and his wounded deputy had appeared, Alice wasn't sure how she and Griffin would go on, but it seemed God had answered her prayers. Their group had found each other again and that alone bolstered her spirits, kept the adrenaline surging through her veins, though she was more terrified than she'd ever been. Still, she did as Sheriff Kruse asked and focused on hiking and leading them out of this disaster.

After a while, though, she couldn't take Griffin's labored breathing. He was assisting Deputy Reed but he had his own injuries to deal with.

She turned on her heel. "Okay, it's my turn

with Deputy Reed. I'll help him now. Just keep hiking in the same general direction."

Griffin's face contorted. "He's becoming deadweight, Alice. You're strong, but I don't think—"

Sheriff Kruse took the man's other side. "Griffin and I can do it together or I'll carry him in a fireman's carry. But I think we're almost there. I can hear the river roaring. Come on, Alice. Let's pick up the pace."

She relinquished Deputy Reed's arm to the sheriff, nodded and got back on track. But the sheriff was right—the sound of a bigger rush of water met her ears and it was the most joyous sound she could remember hearing. Exhausted, driven by fear, she hadn't immediately recognized the sound. But now hope rushed at her and she could run to the river, if it weren't for the slow-moving men behind her.

Through the trees, she spotted the gorge ahead and that chipped away at her joy. It wasn't a straight shot to the river. How could she have forgotten? "We have to hike west to avoid the canyon."

Griffin groaned. "How far?"

"Not too far. A half mile maybe." She winced inside, knowing even that short distance was a long way for an injured man to carry a suffering comrade over rough terrain.

She led them west and away from the brook, to where the river spilled out of the canyon. They still had to face climbing down a short ridge to return to their base camp, but it was their only way in and out of the river. It was the reason they'd chosen that spot. And they were almost back to where they'd started. Relief swelled inside.

Then, finally, Alice stared down at the base camp and soaked in the sight. She could hardly believe it. "We're here." She bent over her thighs. "We made it."

Alice took a moment to catch her breath as she waited on the men. Getting Deputy Reed down wouldn't be easy.

Deputy Edwards, who'd been shot as well, appeared to be recovering and had already packed up camp and loaded the raft. But he'd thought to leave water out for them.

He glanced up when he heard their approach, his face brightening, relief apparent in his demeanor.

Sheriff Kruse appeared by her side and called down, "We're going to need some help. Reed's been shot." The sheriff's words came out breathy. "And we need to hurry. There could be men on our tail."

Deputy Edwards was fresh and ready to work, even with his own gunshot wound, after the hours he'd spent resting. He responded with alacrity and assisted them in getting Deputy Reed down the ridge. Alice could hardly stand to hear the man's groans as the effort caused him more pain. The fact that he was still alive was a good sign, she thought. It meant his gunshot wound hadn't caused him to bleed out. Still, it could be life threatening. At least they still had a chance to get him the medical attention he needed.

At the bottom of the ridge Alice stood on the small beach near the river. She watched the sheriff and Deputy Edwards take a few moments to examine Deputy Reed's injuries and treat his gunshot wound.

"What about you, Griffin?" she asked. "You were shot back there, too."

"It's nothing."

"Let me see." She tried to remove the jacket he'd donned, and caught a glimpse of blood at his side near his waist and gasped.

He shrugged away. "I'm not going to die from it. It just sliced through me, is all. It's already stopped bleeding so you can quit worrying about me."

Alice was taken aback at his sharp, impatient tone.

He glanced to the ridge they'd descended and blew out a breath. "I'm sorry for snapping at you. I'm just anxious to get on the river. Every second we stay here increases our risk. They're hunting us. They could be on us any minute now."

"He's right," Sheriff Kruse said. "I think we've got Reed doctored enough. Let's go."

They quickly scrambled onto the raft. Only Sheriff Kruse and Griffin manned paddles, while the two wounded deputies stayed out of the way, and Alice grabbed her oars, glad to grip them and feel the sense of power and control over her own life once again. She had never been happier to be in a raft on the Rogue River. When she'd started this trip, she'd feared getting back on the water. Feared guiding these men. Her worst fears had occurred when they'd fallen in the water—still, no one had died. And now her perspective had completely flipped.

With confidence and not a little desperation, she guided the raft away from the riverbank and back out into the middle of the Rogue River. The fast-moving river current snatched the raft and carried them away. With each passing mile that put distance between them and the men who hunted them, the tension eased from her shoulders. The farther away from those men they could get, the better. As sheer relief surged, adrenaline crashed and left her with grateful tears that threatened to spill.

Oh, no, no...I can't cry. Not now. She needed to stay in control. They still had miles to go and she was their guide. She'd get home, safe and sound in her own house, before she let herself truly crash. This experience had beaten her spirit and left her brutalized. But she knew it could have been worse, so much worse. She wouldn't let herself blame the sheriff for this. He'd only been doing his job by surveilling things before he called in the big guns. She glanced at him and saw the storm raging in his eyes as he remained alert to their surroundings, to the ridges that might be sheltering possible snipers.

Deputy Edwards, still recovering from his wound from yesterday, remained alert as well, apparently, feeling the same sense of danger and urgency pouring off the sheriff. Deputy Reed's head rested against the raft, his eyes shut.

And Griffin...her heart jumped when she looked at him. Griffin sat slumped over with his head in his hands. That sight could crush her.

She wasn't the only one left splintered.

Driving home that point, other rafts loaded with thrill seekers and a guide or two passed them by as they paddled while Alice let their raft drift with the current. Shouting at them with cheers of victory because they'd made it through those dangerous rapids. Then when the rafters got a good look at the motley crew in her raft, they turned into those rubberneckers on the freeway slowing to gawk at an accident. Bloody and beaten, they presented as an unusual sight on the river.

Ignore them. Just ignore them.

And she did for the most part. Exhausted to the bone, she ran on fumes.

And when the sheriff shifted, his grim features lifted a little as he caught the sight ahead of them. So did hers.

River Ranch Lodge.

Civilization.

Or the closest thing they'd be able to find to it as they floated out of the Wild and Scenic portion of the river, leaving the twists, turns and very real and present dangers, leaving the canyon behind them. Griffin slowly lifted his head and sat taller. He didn't look at Alice. For some reason she'd hoped, or maybe even expected, a glance from him to check on her, at least. Unbidden disappointment curdled in her stomach.

Deputy Edwards appeared expectant. Only Reed had no clue they were nearly to safety.

Alice couldn't guide the raft fast enough as

she steered to the short pier that extended out from the bank.

In the gravel parking lot of the lodge, an ambulance waited.

She glanced at the sheriff.

"I wanted them ready for the eventuality that we would make it out," he said. "I was right to call them."

He almost sounded like he'd said those last words to reassure himself of his decision.

Her eyes narrowed. "You knew we'd run into trouble?"

"I didn't know for sure, but on the off chance that someone was injured, I wanted them waiting for us on the other side of this—today. I trusted you'd get us in and out quickly, and you did just that, Alice, both on the river and in the wilderness. I'm sorry about what you had to go through but I appreciate your help. I don't think it would have turned out the same without you."

Alice wasn't so sure about that, but at least it was over now. That's all she cared about.

The second the raft bumped the dock, two men who'd waited on the riverbank assisted them out and secured the raft, for which Alice was grateful. She stepped out and onto solid ground, wanting to drop and hug the good earth. They'd made it. From there, she moved in a daze as the scene unfolded before her. Medics rushed both wounded deputies onto gurneys and into the ambulance. Others saw to Griffin's gunshot wound, though as he claimed, it hadn't been serious.

At the far end of the gravel lot near law enforcement vehicles, the sheriff shouted at the additional deputies and argued with Oregon State police officers and park rangers. His words were indignant and furious.

What he said, she didn't know. Didn't care.

A woman with the sheriff's department wrapped a blanket around her and ushered her to a bench next to the lodge. She spoke in soft tones, but Alice couldn't seem to understand her words.

Shock...she heard that word. Yes. That was it. Alice thought she just might be in shock. But she didn't want to sit. She felt like she was supposed to do something. When she turned, Griffin approached, a bandage on his forehead—where he'd been pistol-whipped—and another around his waist. Despite the pain she knew he must be feeling from his injuries, he smiled. That deep, sensitive look came into his gray eyes. That same look that had drawn her to him in the first place. Her mind raced, reeling through the horrible events of the last two days and paused at the moment of his tender kiss.

Their terrifying predicament had pushed

them both to the edge, so the kiss hadn't been a promise of more to come. And even if it had been, Alice wouldn't believe that promise. She wouldn't trust Griffin to keep it.

Still, she didn't want him to think she believed they were a "thing" now. She didn't want to lean into him, rely on him. Feel his sturdy form against hers. No. She wanted to show him she was strong. But a girl just needed a hug sometimes. Even Alice, who'd toughened up since Griffin had left her the first time...

And she expected what came next. They'd always had this connection that meant Griffin knew what Alice needed. When he opened his arms, she stepped right into them where she fit perfectly against him.

Moments before, Griffin had studied Alice while the female deputy draped a blanket over her shoulders and asked about injuries. Alice was bruised and exhausted but he imagined that the most serious of her wounds were psychological. Nothing the nice deputy could do for Alice there. He sent up a silent prayer for Deputy Edwards and Deputy Reed, that they healed quickly and for his sheriff uncle who had enough trouble on his hands without having a disagreement with the other law enforcement agencies.

Griffin had been kept out of it, for which he was glad, when he'd been rushed forward and his graze of a gunshot wound tended, cuts and scrapes bandaged. All the while, he'd never taken his eyes from Alice, needing the visual reminder that she was safe. It could have been worse, so much worse.

The look on Alice's face as the woman tried to talk to her had scared him to his core—deep furrows lined her forehead, creased her brow, and yet her gaze was nothing but a blank stare. Her mouth had hung slightly open.

She'd done well to guide them back to that garden and out again, then get them down the river. She'd fulfilled her commitment and had held herself together for as long as they'd needed her. But now that they were there, safe and sound, he could see that the adrenaline was bleeding out of her as she let the shock of it roll over her.

He knew that look all too well. Had seen it happen all too often.

Not here, not in the States, but on foreign soil and the aftermath of a bloodied battle-field. He'd taken pictures, a thousand images of anger, fear, hatred, evil…and shock.

He had a fresh new image that raced across his thoughts, torturing him—Alice being dragged by criminals with utterly evil intentions. She might never be the same, and that scared him for her.

And…for him.

He could have insisted they find another way. Tried harder to come up with a plan that had kept her safe from harm. Something. By now he should be accustomed to the violence and blood of war—whether on insurgents, terrorists or drugs—but Alice should never have been touched by any of that. And the thought of her in that kind of danger made it clear that he wasn't numb to the damage, either.

Regardless, he'd known she needed someone to hold her. And now that she was in his arms, he realized his mistake. *He* was the one who'd needed someone to hold *him*. And not just someone, but Alice. He needed to hold her and feel her tight against him, secure in his arms. He drew her even closer—fitting to him.

Felt the steady rhythm of her heart. The tremble in her body and limbs.

"We made it, Alice. It's going to be okay now." His reassurances fell flat but he didn't have more words than that. There simply were none.

The danger they had faced had been much too close for comfort. They had nearly lost their lives. He sure hoped his uncle didn't make a practice of this kind of operation, but to be fair, this kind of activity on such a large and dangerous scale in the wilderness wasn't the everyday scenario.

Alice continued to hold on to him, and Griffin was there for her however long she needed. He squeezed his eyes shut and grimaced. That...wasn't exactly true. And the truth of it raked over him. He was there for her now, but he wouldn't be sticking around—just like he hadn't before. What...what would have happened two years ago if he hadn't accepted that News Corp assignment in Africa—the excuse he'd needed to run? What would have happened between them if he'd stayed? Would they still be together, their relationship deepened?

Every time that question had snagged him over the last two years, he'd ignored it, dug deeper into whatever project he worked on at the time. It was all a moot point. He didn't stay, he wouldn't have stayed, and he can't stay now.

He relinquished his hold on her when another deputy appeared to usher them into a sheriff's department SUV that would take them back to Gideon. In the backseat, Griffin steeled himself against the exhaustion. Just a little longer...

He gestured for Alice to scoot closer and she did, resting her head against his shoulder. Griffin was surprised when his uncle climbed into the front passenger seat.

"What are you doing?" Griffin asked. "Aren't you headed in the opposite direction?"

His uncle shifted around to face them. "I'm not riding with you, but you tried to talk to me earlier on the hike out. What did you want to tell me?"

Griffin had started to fill his uncle in on what had happened to them, but he hadn't wanted to distract Alice from leading them back out, or scare her with his words, so had decided to wait. And now, he'd prefer to have this conversation privately, away from her, but he might not get another chance and his uncle needed to know everything that had occurred.

"Back there we were on the ridge, on a terrace. From there I could see a lot. Wished I could have warned you. You could have come back and Deputy Reed might not have gotten shot. But then someone was up on the ridge behind us and tried to kill us. I knocked him unconscious and we escaped. We climbed up and over the ridge and another pair of men followed us. Finally caught up with us. They…" He glanced down at Alice where she leaned against him. Hadn't wanted to talk about it in front of her "…they wanted her alive. They came after us because they wanted her so they could take her back to someone."

"Whoever that someone is," she said.

"My point is that Alice is still in danger. It's more than them wanting her dead so she couldn't show us the way. There's something more at play here."

"Maybe they wanted to silence her at first, and now that it's too late they want revenge," his uncle said. "But beyond that, she's going to remember who that guy is eventually. Give us his name. She's the witness."

"Whatever the reason, she'll be in danger until we take these men down."

His uncle took the news in with a grim nod. "I'll station a deputy in Gideon with her while we go back in to shut the operation down—loaded for bear this time. Go get some rest tonight, Griffin. I'll text you about when to expect me or someone from the department to pick you up, but I'm pretty sure it'll be predawn hours."

"I have my own ride. Just let me know when and where to meet you."

Alice shifted away from him and glanced up at Griffin, searching. Hurt and anger gathered like a storm in her eyes. He'd known the news would upset her, and this wasn't how he'd wanted her to learn that he would go back in for the story. He'd wanted to talk it through with her, make sure she understood. He needed to go back in—it was the whole reason he'd come in the first place. What did she expect?

And she also had to know that after he got everything he needed for the story, he would leave.

Again.

ELEVEN

Deputy Cosgrove finally steered the SUV into Gideon well after supper time. Alice directed him over to the Wilderness, Inc. office where he parked. Though her stomach grumbled, she was too tired to eat. She stumbled out of the vehicle wanting nothing more than a long hot shower and a soft bed. People stopped and gawked at the law enforcement vehicle spilling its contents—a bedraggled man and woman, and one frustrated sheriff's deputy who would have to babysit her until this was over.

That had been the longest ride of her life through the curvy mountain roads that made her nauseous. All she wanted was to be clean again and to sleep forever. The grueling drive had been worsened by all the emotional angst twisting through her at the thought of Griffin going back in to that terror in the wilderness. Or any of the law enforcement men and women venturing into that firestorm.

At least this time they'd be armed and prepared. But would it be enough against criminals so ruthless and determined? Alice hadn't stopped shaking. She was pretty sure she'd kept that hidden, but if pushed too far, it would become all too obvious. She wanted to forget the terror she'd just experienced. After running for her life twice in those woods, how could she ever look at them the same? Or go hiking and not be afraid?

What was she going to do? Griffin approached, his lips pursed and brows furrowed. She'd never seen him look more haggard. And yet, relief shone behind his gray-eyed gaze.

She sucked in a breath. They'd made it out. But… Griffin was going back in.

He loosely grabbed her arms. "We both need some rest. I'm going to crash on the sofa at the Wilderness, Inc.—"

"No."

Hurt flashed in his eyes. "Oh?"

"I mean, no, you're not going to crash on the couch. Take the bed in the apartment. Since I have a deputy to watch over me now, I'll stay in my own home. You need a real bed to get any kind of meaningful rest. Especially since you have an early morning."

For the life of her, she didn't know why he'd come back to Gideon at all today instead of heading off to Gold Beach with his uncle. Part of her wanted to believe it had something to do with her, but then she remembered his high-speed motorcycle. That made sense. He'd come back for that and would ride it to Gold Beach. She was sure.

His frown deepened, and she thought he would say more, but he nodded and released her. He left her to speak to Cosgrove who waved his hands around while he talked with a few men from Gideon. No one smiled. All eyes turned to Alice.

Oh, Lord, please... She didn't want their attention. Were they angry with her for bringing danger to their town? Or concerned for her? She assumed the deputy warned them of the situation and to be on the lookout for strangers who might hurt Alice or others in Gideon.

Griffin and Deputy Cosgrove shared a few words as they glanced at her. She should be in the middle of that conversation but she was too exhausted to care what they were saying. Still, she walked around the SUV to join Griffin and the deputy. "Listen, I'm just going to head on over to the house, okay?"

She had so much to say to Griffin, and at the same time nothing to say at all. She didn't want him to go back in there. Wished that none of them had to go. But she wouldn't beg him this time. And besides, it wasn't like they had been dating again. No. They just had this strange connection that went far beyond the physical and she couldn't seem to shake that, no matter how hard she tried.

And once he went off to get those pictures of a wilderness battlefield with an army of weed growers, would he come back and at least tell her goodbye? Or would he just disappear from her life again? She knew the answer to her question so why bother asking.

"Hold on, Alice. Let me check the house first," the deputy said.

She glanced at Griffin. "You still have the extra key to the Wilderness office?"

"Yep. I'll return it when I'm done, don't worry."

Alice turned her back on him before she lost it.

Once the deputy had checked her home, every nook and cranny, every closet and room, Alice released a sigh. She forced herself to eat a bowl of soup and crackers, then showered and slipped into bed, trusting the deputy to guard the house while she slept.

Pain rippled up her arm as Griffin tugged her deeper into the woods, but no matter how hard and fast they ran, they couldn't move fast enough through the trees. Their pursuers gained on them. Gunfire exploded near her ears and bullets whizzed past. Men's voices ricocheted all around her like bullets from an automatic weapon, but she couldn't see them. Only sense them—and the danger they brought with them—drawing near, getting closer.

Griffin held on tighter and pulled harder but Alice's hand slipped from his. He disappeared into the darkness ahead. She called his name. Heard him call back, searching for her, but it was no use.

Alice was alone, running from the darkness, from these men who were evil incarnate.

The man she'd met, the man who knew her stepped in front of her, his dark eyes piercing. I know you.

I know you…I know you…

But I don't *know* you. Who are you?

He pulled Griffin out of the darkness and held a gun to his head.

And fired.

Alice bolted upright in bed. Drenched in sweat, she gasped for breath. Her heart pounded as if it wanted to escape her chest. She waited for her breathing to calm and her heartbeat to finally slow.

"It was only a dream." But it felt so real, and the vivid images remained. "It was only a dream," she repeated, as if to convince herself.

She looked at the clock. Three in the morning.

"Griffin," she whispered into the moonlit room.

And threw the covers off. Alice moved to the window to glance through the blinds. Through the woods that surrounded her house, she could see her deputy bodyguard. He stood closer to the buildings in town than to her house, as he spoke with another man. She could just make out their silhouettes.

Griffin.

He was obviously prepared to head back into the battle for his pictures, the story he would write to expose these atrocities. It was worse than dangerous. So what if he'd served in battles on foreign soil, gathering stories for the government? This situation was more than hazardous to his health. She couldn't shake the images of him dying in *her* wilderness. A sickness twisted around in her stomach, turning to nausea.

She had a bad feeling about this. A very. Bad. Feeling.

She cared about Griffin's safety. There was nothing irrational in that, was there? He'd nearly been killed before during his last tour in Iraq and had received a traumatic brain injury.

Right. Why couldn't she be honest with herself? Her concern for him went much deeper than that. He reminded her of what she'd been missing in her life. He made her smile. And— she swallowed the sudden knot in her throat— made her happy. If he was killed, all of what they had together would die with him. But the sad truth of it was the happiness she felt with him couldn't last, even if he survived. He wouldn't stick around to keep making her happy. It was a moot point to even think about it. Why couldn't she let it go?

And even if he chose to stay, how could she *ever* trust him? What if she let herself fall hard for him and he pulled what she now thought of as "a Griffin" and he left again, never to come back?

Alice shook off all her melancholy, her ridiculously selfish thoughts. She couldn't let him go without trying to stop him, even though she knew in her heart what he would say. If it would save his life, she had to try.

One. Last. Time.

While his uncle spoke with Cosgrove over his cell phone, Griffin eyed Alice's house through the trees. Deputy Cosgrove had been staked out tonight to protect her, and part of Griffin resented him for it. Protecting Alice was supposed to be his job. But his uncle had assigned the job to Cosgrove, and Griffin hadn't protested. He needed to rest if he were going to get his pictures, but he hadn't been ready to let go of her yet. Guilt clenched Griffin's gut. There'd been so much more he'd wanted—no, *needed*—to say to Alice before he left.

But he was a coward. Didn't want to face her. He wouldn't come back here after it was over. There wasn't any point. Seeing her one last time would only prolong the inevitable. His departure. They had no future together.

Still…

"Griffin, sheriff wants to know why you haven't left yet," Deputy Cosgrove said.

"Tell him I'll leave in a minute."

Cosgrove repeated the words, though his uncle likely heard his comment over the phone. "He says you have ten."

Griffin nodded. It was only thirty-five miles to Gold Beach where he would meet the rest of the team but would take him an hour on the twisted road. He wasn't sure why his uncle had even called his deputy. Maybe it was to check up on Griffin to make sure he headed out as promised. Or maybe his uncle thought Cosgrove should know the plans in case he was called upon to assist. Surely it wouldn't come to that. If it did, Alice would be left alone.

Should someone call one or both of her brothers? Her father? Try to reach them? They never liked Griffin or trusted him with Alice because they knew he wasn't commitment material, but once they found out what was going on in their absence they would be well and truly angry no one had contacted them regarding Alice's role in this and the danger she was in. And now that he thought about it, he should have called Cooper at the beginning, when he'd first arrived in Gideon and Alice believed someone had followed her. She was in danger. Her family had the right to be informed. He finally admitted he'd been selfish not to call them, wanting to be the one she relied on, but he hadn't recognized that before.

While he pondered these thoughts, Griffin hiked up the path to her house. Did the deputy understand just how much danger Alice was in? Was Griffin making a mistake in leaving her in someone else's hands?

A twig snapped. Leaves rustled. He paused and listened. Then stepped off the path into the trees. Tugged his weapon out. Waited. A chill crawled over him. Was someone out there waiting for his chance to get at Alice?

He'd check the perimeter, just to make sure she would be all right. No matter there'd been a deputy assigned her for tonight.

What had he heard?

Something moved in his peripheral vision.

Pointing his weapon, Griffin swiveled to face the threat.

The deputy approached from behind. "What are you doing? I've already done this. Been here all night. There's no one out there."

"I thought I heard something. You don't mind if I check again, do you?"

Cosgrove snorted. "Be my guest. I'll come along."

Griffin and the deputy walked around the house. Looked for evidence someone had been here. But they found nothing. Once they were back around front and on the path again, Griffin tucked his weapon away.

"I guess I overreacted. Thought I heard something." And he hoped that was it.

"Just a case of the nerves. And she's fine, by the way."

"I'm going to talk to her before I leave, if you don't mind." Yeah. He would talk to her before he left. One last time.

The deputy didn't move.

Griffin tucked his chin. Gave him a look he hoped the man would understand.

Finally he seemed to register Griffin's meaning. "Oh! Right. I'll…uh…give you some privacy."

Griffin waited until Deputy Cosgrove had walked the length of the path before working up the nerve to approach her door. Uncle Davis had given him ten minutes, but the patrol had eaten into that. He was probably down to five now.

He lifted his hand to knock. It was after three in the morning. He'd be waking her and likely from a deep sleep. Dread filled his insides. What did he think he was doing? What was he going to say to her? But leaving without saying goodbye had wrong written all over it.

The door swung open before he knocked and she rushed through, almost running him over.

"Griffin!" She backed away, appearing stunned to see him. "I…I saw you outside. I was just on my way out to tell you goodbye."

"Alice…" He wanted to take her in his arms. But why? Why would he torture either of them like that? He had to be strong for the both of them. "I came to say goodbye, too. I should have done it last night, but we were both exhausted and I didn't know what to say."

"I lied just now. I didn't come to say goodbye. Not exactly."

"Oh?" The moon moved behind a cloud and darkness grew stark around them.

"I came out to warn you. Griffin, please don't go back in there. I don't want you to get hurt."

"We've already talked about this. I can take care of myself. You know my history." He'd been discharged when he'd received that traumatic brain injury, but his training had never left him. "This wouldn't be the first time I've dealt with a dangerous situation."

She grabbed his hand then. Weaved her fingers with his. The feel of her soft skin along with the desperation pouring off her had a powerful effect on him. Would she beg? *Oh no, please don't do this, Alice...* And would he say the words she wanted to hear again, just like before, only to appease her?

He willed the wall up, but it was getting more difficult to protect himself, to ignore the feelings she ignited in him.

"This isn't the same. This wilderness region, these are *my* woods. I can't stand the thought of something worse happening than what I've already been through. It's selfish, I know, but Griffin, you can't die in *my* woods."

A short laugh escaped. "Oh, so I just have to make sure I die somewhere else?" He tried to tease her but it fell flat. "I'm sorry, I shouldn't have said that. I know it's serious. I know that. But this time, we're going in with plenty of firepower."

Sighing, she leaned against the door. Crossed her arms.

Griffin looked up at the tree canopy, searching for what stars he could find in the gaps when the clouds released the moon again. "Look, I came to see you before I went. You knew I was going." She'd had hours in the vehicle with him on the long drive back to Gideon yesterday to talk about this. "Why are you reacting this way? It isn't a surprise."

She pressed her face in her hands. Just as he reached out she dropped her hands. He dropped his.

"I had a bad dream. A nightmare."

"I'm sorry." After everything she'd been through, a nightmare wasn't a surprise, and he wanted to hold her, comfort her. "I understand about those. Sometimes I even have what feels like a nightmare going on in my head when I'm wide-awake."

"You mean because of what you've seen as a combat photographer?"

"Yeah, and from the jobs I've taken other places in the world. Kenya. Mexico." In truth, he'd seen nothing here that could compare, and he hoped the next few hours wouldn't change that.

"It's just that…I have a bad feeling about this, Griffin." She leaned into him then, pressing her fists against his chest but held back from a full-on hug. "I'm not going to beg you to stay. I'm not going to humiliate myself like that. We aren't *together* like we were before.

But I'm going to ask you, as a friend, *please* don't go."

His spirits sank. *Oh, Lord.*

This was just like what happened two years ago. Her pleas twisted him into knots, just like before. Even though, like she said, they weren't romantically involved now. But maybe they had fooled themselves on that count. One didn't have to officially date to be emotionally invested. The feelings were still there, the whole time, but they both ignored them when they could, skirted them when they couldn't ignore them.

In the shadows, there was just enough light for him to see her eyes glistening. He'd never seen her cry when he'd known her before. This experience had changed her.

It had changed him because he'd watched her go through it. "I wish that I'd met you in another time and place. I can't change who I am or what I do. Documenting the brutality of war zones, whether militarized or otherwise, is all I've ever done. It's all I know, even now as a private citizen. There's no real decision to be made here. No real choice." He shouldn't do it. He really shouldn't do it. But he encircled her neck with his hands, weaved his fingers into her soft hair. And here he was positioned to kiss her—and he wanted that more than he had a right—so now what? A kiss at this point could devastate them both.

Instead, he pressed his forehead to hers. Smiled a little, hoping to elicit the same from her. She sniffled and returned it.

"I'm sorry," he said. "I didn't mean to show up here and hurt you again, if that's what I've done." She was as solid as a person could be, but her heart was tender. Vulnerable.

"I'm not hurt. You're not hurting me. I mean, how can I be hurt? But I *am* scared for you, and for those law enforcement officers that will have to go back in and clean the vermin out of the woods. And that doesn't have to be you. You're wrong, you know. You do have a choice. You can make a different decision this time."

The crunch of footfalls coming up the path told him his time was running out. He kissed her forehead, and felt like he left a piece of his heart behind in that simple gesture.

Griffin let her go and walked away from her to go get his story.

Trying, and failing, to ignore the ache in his heart. He hoped she understood why he couldn't come back.

TWELVE

You do have a choice. You can make a different decision this time.

His leather jacket zipped tight, the wind blasted around him as he took the twisted mountain road from Gideon to Gold Beach in the early morning hours.

This was it. This was the whole reason he had this high-speed motorcycle. So he could get lost in the rush of riding and forget his pain. The sheer effort it took to focus on the road pulled his thoughts away from Alice's words. Well, it was supposed to. Thinking about her could be a distraction that would get him killed, but he couldn't get her out of his mind and heart.

A buck dashed across the road in front of him, and he swerved dangerously close to the edge, then slowed, letting three does join the buck. Heart pounding, he steered back on the road.

Focus. Somehow, he had to focus. But it was no use trying to push thoughts of Alice away.

He'd always wondered what would have happened if he hadn't left for Kenya—or if he'd come back, as he'd said he would. Regardless, he wasn't relationship material. His head was too messed up. She deserved so much more than he could offer. So much better.

A little over an hour later, Griffin steered his motorcycle into a parking lot filled with law enforcement vehicles from multiple counties, including the Oregon State Police—the command center, as it were—and two helicopters.

His uncle approached him. He was easy enough to spot pulling in on his motorcycle. Griffin removed his helmet.

"Stay here so I can find you," his uncle said. "You'll likely be with me."

Then he left Griffin to get back to coordinating the group. Griffin got off his motorcycle, unpacked his camera and took photographs of the gathering storm of law enforcement for at least an hour. He couldn't use them all but he'd taken some powerful shots, he was sure. This story could very well make as profound an exposé as any he'd documented in combat zones.

They prepared to wage a large-scale battle, and it propelled Griffin back into the action again. His heart rate kicked up a few notches.

He squeezed his eyes shut as memories of images and sounds from his past crashed through him.

Multiple rapid-fire weapons resounded. Men barked orders. A hummer exploded twenty-five yards from him.

And the more recent near-death experience he'd gone through with Alice. The mental picture of the men dragging her away remained far too vivid. Too raw.

He scraped a hand over his still-tired features. Then this morning… If only he could delete the snapshot in his head of her pleading with him.

But there was something else. Something wasn't right. Something was out of place and gnawed at the back of his mind. It gave him the sense that he should listen to her this time and walk away.

Not go with these men into the war zone.

Except he'd be giving up a story. A good story. The whole reason he'd come to Gideon, Oregon, and faced Alice again. His sheriff uncle and his multicounty, multiagency task force were about to descend on a seriously large marijuana growing operation worth tens of millions of dollars and he had the chance to cover the story from the front line.

Could he really give that up?

God, please help me to make the right decision here! I don't know what to do.

He'd never walked away from a scoop, and this was exactly what he'd been looking for. The point of no return came all too quickly. He needed to make a decision. The troops started moving out.

Uncle Davis approached him again. Crossed his arms and gave Griffin a piercing look. "I can't have you with us if you're not one hundred percent in. Don't need your blood on my hands. Your mother would have my head. Besides, I kind of like you. Wouldn't want to lose you. You've made me proud all these years, so it's not like anyone would be disappointed in you if you chose not to go this time."

"What are you talking about? Of course I'm one hundred percent in."

"You're distracted. I'd have to be blind not to see it."

Griffin didn't know what to say to that. Was he that obvious?

"Don't worry. Even if you stay behind, you'll get the story, whatever I can give you. I'm just not a photographer."

His uncle was giving him an out. What if Griffin made a different decision this time? A different choice? Just for the sake of changing things up. Maybe Alice was right. Though he'd always been compelled to expose the truth, he *did* have a choice.

He shook his head. "I don't know why, but I think I need to sit this one out. Maybe you should, too." He'd seen enough carnage to last a lifetime. And frankly, he was tired of it. There was a chance this whole exercise could go smoothly, with no one hurt—but based on the violence they'd encountered when approaching the operation the day before, that hardly seemed likely. The chances were high that someone would get hurt or worse, killed. But he sure hoped it didn't come to that—for his uncle's sake, and all the law enforcement involved.

"Thought so. But I'm needed in the thick of it, you understand."

Griffin nodded. "I know. I've wasted enough of your time. I don't know what it is. I just have this feeling I need to walk away."

"And go back for the girl, I get it."

His uncle's words surprised him, though he didn't know why. They had him backpedaling. He shook his head. "It's not like that."

"Right, well I kind of hoped you were going back to Gideon. Deputy Cosgrove will need a break after standing watch all night. I don't have anyone else to spare. But if you're not heading that way…"

"I am. But not for the reasons you think." Back at Alice's house, he was sure he'd heard something. Sensed someone watching, even though Cosgrove had assured him no one was there and their patrol hadn't turned up any evidence of a trespasser. And he couldn't ignore the gnawing in the back of his mind, too—he needed to trust his instincts this time, and they told him to listen to Alice and stay behind, and not for the reasons *she* thought—that Griffin was in danger and might die if he went on the raid—but because Alice was in danger.

"If you don't want to ride your motorcycle, you can take these." His uncle held out the keys to his department vehicle. "Your bike will be safe here. I'll pick my vehicle and you up in Gideon when it's over."

Was his uncle nuts? "Why would I want to take your vehicle when mine is faster?"

His uncle angled his head and gave him a warning look. "That's what I was worried about. If you're in a hurry to get back, I don't want you on that thing. It's dangerous."

Griffin gripped his uncle's hand, but didn't take the keys. "No, thanks. I'm good. But be careful out there."

His uncle nodded. "Same goes for you, Griffin. Be careful protecting Alice, and try not to get hurt." With those words he jogged over to a waiting helicopter.

Had there been a double meaning in his words?

Griffin climbed back onto his Hayabusa, but before he donned his helmet he had something to do. He'd noted Cooper's cell phone number while in the man's office in case he needed to make the call. He should have done it much sooner, but Alice hadn't wanted to, and even his uncle had made no effort to contact Alice's family. Maybe he'd learn that Cooper or Gray couldn't return fast enough, Griffin didn't know. But he owed it to them to at least tell them what was going on. And even if the man was deep in the woods with no signal, he could leave a message.

And wouldn't Cooper Wilde be surprised to hear from Griffin, especially with the story he had to tell? Surprised and angry, very angry.

The deed done, he hung his head. "What am I *doing*?"

He'd told Alice before that the story wasn't his priority even though the images, the story, had *always* taken precedence. But it had all shifted with Alice in danger, and he had the very real sense that she was in danger right this minute. More peril than they knew.

He peeled out of the parking lot, that sense

burning in his gut that he'd better hurry. His uncle wouldn't like it, but Griffin had made the right choice to stick with his motorcycle.

Five thirty in the morning arrived much too early, especially after tossing and turning since she'd heard Griffin's motorcycle rumble out of Gideon. Alice realized she would never fall back to sleep so she got up and pulled on a hoodie over the T-shirt and sweats she'd slept in. Then left her house, woke poor Deputy Cosgrove up in his vehicle and explained that she was headed to the Wilderness, Inc. offices. He appeared embarrassed that he'd fallen asleep. Though she was jealous he could sleep so easily, she didn't blame him for getting some shut-eye.

Poor guy. Staying up all night to watch out for her had to be the worst job ever. After the good deputy made sure she was safe inside the office, he left her alone. She brewed coffee and took a cup to where the deputy sat on the bench outside. Alice made herself comfortable at the desk in Cooper's office and yawned. Of course. *Now* she grew sleepy. She filled her second cup of black coffee. She was on a mission now and couldn't allow herself to fall asleep like the deputy had at some point.

Why had this occurred while her family, her

support system, her friends, were all gone? She couldn't wait until everyone returned so she could share about her experiences. She needed someone there to commiserate with her while she waited and prayed for those descending into the evil in the woods.

Still, in the meantime, until the battle was over, she could be proactive. She could look through the photographs like Sheriff Kruse had suggested. Try to forget that Griffin and his uncle were heading back into the infested wilderness, even though they had plenty of law enforcement backup this time.

Still, Griffin's departure this morning bothered her more than it should, and certainly not for the same reason this time as it had the last time.

When he'd walked away from her before, Alice had thought she'd been in love. And even when he'd left, she'd believed he would come back as soon as he could. She'd been too trusting and too naive, and had gotten her heart broken as a result. No wonder Cooper and Gray had hated the guy.

She'd had no idea that waiting and wondering when Griffin would return from Kenya would be so devastating, so agonizing until Cooper had taken her aside and explained that he'd spoken with the sheriff months after his departure and learned that Griffin had moved on to another story from Kenya. The sheriff had been quite frank—he didn't expect Griffin back anytime soon. Her brother had to deliver the awful painful truth of it. Griffin hadn't died. No. He was fine and dandy living his life away from Gideon and Alice.

Alice had been crushed.

The thought of it still made her furious, absolutely furious—more so with herself than with Griffin. She'd forced him to say the words—that he would return—to appease her. Had he ever had any intention of following through on them? How could she let him put his arms around her this time? Kiss her, even. How could she let herself worry about him? She *knew* better when it came to having feelings for that man. Yet even though he hadn't come back to Gideon until three days ago—and for motives that had nothing to do with Alice—she sensed he still cared.

She groaned, hating how pathetic she was. If only she hadn't had the bad dream that had left her with a sense of dread and followed her around all morning.

God, please keep them safe. "And please help me to get over Griffin, once and for all."

She accepted that he wouldn't come back

to Gideon once he had his story. She wouldn't see him again.

And I'm okay with that. I have to be.

He'd hurt her to the point where she could never trust him, so she had to let him go. Again.

It was for the best. Griffin was no good for her and never had been. She wished he hadn't shown up in Gideon to begin with, stirring up all those feelings from their past. Igniting the battle inside her over wanting to be in his arms safe and warm even knowing he wasn't the guy for her.

Regardless, she was terrified for him and the others. When she lifted the mug to her lips, her hand trembled and coffee spilled on the desk.

This ordeal couldn't be over fast enough. In the meantime, she could do her part and see if the man in the wilderness who seemed to know her had been a Wilderness, Inc. client. If so, his picture should be in their files, both physical and digital.

That had to be how he knew her. Someone with Wilderness, Inc. must have guided him at some point. It could have been Alice because his face had been familiar to her somehow.

Before she looked at the pictures, she closed her eyes to once again envision that first moment when she'd peered through the trees and seen the evidence. Then turned to flee and encountered the man who stood in her path. His dark hair, silver at the temples. She hadn't expected the image in her mind would increase her breaths and heart rate with fear and mounting adrenaline as if she were in the moment here and now.

She opened her eyes and flipped through the pages, browsing each photograph of tourists getting into boats, of the boats going down the rapids or of their clients standing in groups— friends, couples, families or even strangers huddled together for photographs before their big wilderness adventure.

A picture grabbed her attention, drawing her eye to the man in the middle of the group. She focused in on him. That river trip had been seared on her mind. She'd never forget it, or his face. The river had dumped the raft, and he'd drowned.

Alice squeezed her eyes shut wishing the memory away. It never should have happened. To this day, she wasn't even sure what had caused the raft to hit the Picket Fence and bounce them out, the raft then turning over. He'd somehow gotten pinned under a rock.

She'd been at it for more than an hour when a noise startled her. It came from out in the store where they sold wilderness gear and camping supplies. At this time of the morning, it might be someone going on a last-minute fishing trip. She'd opened up the store early for that reason. She left the office.

"Can I help you?" she asked as she walked out into the store. Odd, she didn't see anyone there. Where was the customer hiding?

Something clanked to her left. Her pulse jumped. Beyond the emergency medical supply kits, Deputy Cosgrove stepped into view and held up a fishing vest. "I think I'll take this."

"Hey there, you scared me."

"Got tired of sitting outside. Can't stay in the SUV anymore after spending all night in there. Mind if I just hang out at the store?"

"I have a better idea. Let's head over to Ricky's Rogue Bar-B-Q. Bubba usually has bacon and eggs ready for the early birds. You could probably use some more coffee."

He nodded. "Sounds like a plan. And, yeah, I need that coffee black and strong."

"You know, I feel really bad the sheriff left you to babysit—especially for such a long shift. Is he going to send someone so you can get some rest? I don't see how you guys can stay up all night like that."

He ran a hand through his hair and replaced his deputy's hat. "I hope he does, but I wouldn't know who. We're short on deputies as it is without having to take out a marijuana operation.

But don't worry. I'm good for it. You're safe with me. This'll be over in the next day or two, depending on how long it takes the team to get in there. And then you can get back to life without a 'babysitter,' as you put it."

Oh. Well, now, she'd just insulted him.

"Come on." She led him out the door and locked it behind her. "And just so you know, I don't really think of you as a babysitter. I'm sorry I said that. I appreciate that you're watching out for me in case that creep comes looking for me again."

A chill ran over her. She tugged her jacket tighter, even though it wasn't that kind of cold. Alice walked with Deputy Cosgrove to the restaurant and they found seats sitting out on the deck outside before it got too warm. Plenty of others had filled the seats on the deck already—a mix of people Alice had known for years and strangers, tourists who'd come to enjoy the region. Their waitress, a fiftyish, bubbly woman named Tina Jacobs, took their orders of bacon, eggs and pancakes and poured two mugs of steaming coffee.

The aroma of breakfast wafted around her. Alice was suddenly ravenous. She'd expended a ton of energy over the last several days and hadn't replaced her energy stores—she'd been too exhausted. Now it hit her.

Deputy Cosgrove's cell phone rang. He glanced at it. "Would you excuse me? I'll just be right over there."

Frowning slightly, she nodded. "Sure. You go ahead."

A minute or two passed before Tina returned and set Alice's platter before her.

"Wow, that was fast."

"We're already cooking it up to serve, obviously. It's good it's so crowded. I like to keep busy." Tina eyed the empty spot as she set the deputy's loaded platter down.

"Oh, he'll be right back," Alice said. "And, Tina, would you mind bringing us a carafe of black coffee? We've both been up half the night and looks like it's going to be a long day."

"You got it."

Alice glanced around the crowded deck and then through the door into the dining room where other customers sat at tables, but she couldn't see the deputy. She knew he hadn't gone far to take his call, but she worried that the call was something about the raid. Had he walked away because he hadn't wanted her to hear the conversation, in case it was bad news?

Her heart tumbled. *No, Lord, please just let the sheriff, deputies and all those policemen get control of the garden without being injured. Destroy it, and arrest those men.*

And please, Lord, protect...protect Griffin. You know, I care about him. Like my brothers. All those men were important and while she didn't want to pray for favors, one man's safety over another's, she couldn't help herself. God knew her heart anyway.

Just let him be okay and then move on to get the next story.

I...I don't want to see him again.

She couldn't believe she'd actually prayed such a thing. But, yeah. She didn't want to ever see Griffin again. She wasn't sure what it was about him, but she found him irresistible. And she *must* resist. Alice was strong except when she was near Griffin. Then she turned to mush. Okay, so there was one good reason for her brothers to be far from here—so they wouldn't see her in this weakened state.

Alice had to redirect her thoughts to someone or something besides Griffin. She looked around for the deputy. What was taking him so long?

Tina returned and brought the carafe.

"Have you seen the deputy?" Alice asked.

"I saw him back there on his phone a while ago. You want me to go check?"

Concern spread through her. "Yes, please."

Alice took a sip of her coffee and over the rim of her cup her gaze fell on a man sitting at a table in the corner. Dark hair, silver at the temples. Close-cropped beard. Just like a lot of men, except...

It was him. The man with the beard from the woods.

Her heart skipped a few beats. Her breath caught in her throat. Moisture slicked her palms.

Calm down. Just calm down. She had to act like she hadn't seen him. She let her gaze drift slowly away to other customers. Alice finished drinking as if nothing had happened, trying to hide the tremble that had overtaken her hands. Great. Just great. She couldn't hide that she'd spotted him. Still, would he do anything to her with so many people around? But what if he did? She definitely didn't want him to start shooting and others get hurt because of her.

Tina returned. "I'm sorry, hon, but I don't see your deputy anywhere."

And she'd had to say that right in front of the bad guy. Alice forced her breathing to slow. "Thanks, Tina. I'll just go check for myself."

Alice put her napkin on the table and got up. "Oh, and please leave our plates. I'll be right back to finish."

Let the guy think she was coming back.

Once she stepped back inside Ricky's, a full panic set in. She ran to the bathrooms and searched both stalls. Where could he be? Alice gasped for breath. Maybe he had to go back to where he'd parked his vehicle in front of Wilderness, Inc. for some reason and thought she'd be safe at Ricky's. Well, she wasn't. And neither was anyone else inside.

Alice burst through the exit and sprinted around behind the houses so the man wouldn't see her from the deck. By the time she made the office, she was out of breath. Deputy Cosgrove's vehicle sat there empty.

She unlocked the storefront door hoping he was inside. Oh wait. The door was locked. The deputy couldn't be inside. What should she do?

Oh, God, please...

She stepped inside the store and moved to the phone on the counter to call someone. Anyone. But who? She had no idea. The sheriff and all his men were probably still making their way to that devastation in the wilderness even now.

"Deputy Cosgrove, where are you?" She didn't even have his cell phone number. How ridiculous was that? But he wasn't supposed to leave her alone.

Alice locked the door behind her. Pressed her back against the wall and gulped for air. When had she ever been this scared? When she ran from those men in the woods? No. Adrenaline had kicked in then and propelled her forward so she could escape. But here? She was trapped. Yet she knew that she couldn't let the fear take over like this or she was a dead woman.

She gripped the phone handset. *Think. You have to think.* Alice squeezed her eyes shut. Cooper…he couldn't make it in time to help. Nor Griffin, or anyone else. What good was a protector if when she needed him he was nowhere to be found?

Alice was on her own.

THIRTEEN

Someone knocked on the door. Fear shattered through her. She sucked in too much oxygen, then couldn't get enough air. Where was that paper sack?

"Alice?" a familiar voice called out, muffled through the door.

Deputy Cosgrove? But it didn't sound exactly like him. More like Griffin. Okay, now she was really losing it. What had the bad guy sounded like again? She reimagined his words to her.

I do know you.

Alice leaned forward to peek between the fishing vests Deputy Cosgrove had been looking at earlier. Were her eyes deceiving her, playing a painful joke on her terrified mind? She rubbed them.

No. They weren't playing tricks. Through the pane glass window in the door, she saw Griffin on the other side, peering in.

"Griffin?" she rushed forward and unlocked

the door. What could it mean that he was here? Why had he come back?

That realization sank in. *Oh...he came back!*

He smiled at her through the glass. That smile could do some damage. Only it quickly shifted into a frown—probably when he realized how shaken she looked. When she opened the door, she yanked him inside. And then, without thinking, she found herself in his arms. She'd done it. She'd rushed into his arms, again, but he held her as if he missed her and wanted her there forever. Why hadn't he done this years ago? Turned around and come back to her?

But he hadn't. And this wasn't then. They weren't a couple. She wasn't falling for him.

Regaining her composure, she stepped out of his arms. "What are you doing here?"

"How come you ask me that every time I show up?" His eyes narrowed. "What's going on, Alice? What's happened? Where's Cosgrove?"

"You first."

"Fine. I was worried about you so I came back." Something behind his gaze told her it was more.

"You were worried about *me*?" Was she dreaming? Hoping and wishing for a reality she could never have with him. "I was worried about *you*. And not just a little surprised you came back to Gideon. I figured once you got your story, then you were gone. I'd never see you again." *Shut up now, before you reveal just how vulnerable you are, stupid girl.*

He stared at her, appearing stunned and confused, so she continued. "Is the raid over already? What happened?"

He shook his head like shaking off a daze. "No, Alice. You've got it all wrong. It's not over. It hasn't even started yet. The task force is heading into the woods now. It'll take them time to get there. Too much time, as far as I'm concerned."

"I don't understand. What are you doing here, then?"

"You told me I had a choice. I never realized that before."

"You're kidding, right?"

A sardonic grin slid over his face. "Not entirely. I've never let anyone or anything stand in the way of getting what I needed for the story to expose the wrongs in the world."

She crossed her arms. "Are you saying that I stood in your way?" Alice tried not to let hope infuse her voice. Because she couldn't hope. She couldn't trust this man. What was he playing at now?

"Part of getting the story means listening to that sixth sense, or that gut instinct. And today, something told me to come back. I don't know if it was your dream or what, but I just had this sense of dread, so here I am. Looks like I made the right decision. Where's the deputy?"

Alice locked the door, then tugged Griffin deeper into the store. "I don't know. We were at Ricky's Bar-B-Q and he left to take a call. Then I saw the guy."

Griffin gripped her shoulders. "What? You mean the guy from the woods?"

"Yes. He's here, Griffin!" Alice calmed herself. "He's here."

His hands squeezed her tighter before releasing her. She could tell the news shocked him just like it had shocked her. He paced the small space. "Why isn't he with his operation now, preparing to face the authorities? He has to know what's going down." His gaze shifted back to her. "There's only one reason he would be in Gideon. He's here for you, Alice. It's just as I feared. I was right to come back."

"What if he's been here the whole time? What if he lives in Gideon? Why wouldn't I know that, if he did?"

"Exactly. You would have seen him already."

"But I can't know everyone in town. Still, maybe that's why his face is familiar."

"It doesn't matter if he lives here or not. He's here now and he knows you and that you can connect him to that massive illegal operation. Did he follow you when you left the restaurant?"

"I tried to get away without anyone seeing me, but I can't be sure. He could know we're both inside."

Griffin continued pacing again. Ran his hands through his hair. "Let me think. Let me think."

"We need to find the deputy. I mean, now that you're here. Before…I just huddled up in that corner like—" frowning and ashamed, she shook her head "—like a chicken."

Griffin stopped his incessant pacing. Man, she hated to see how this frazzled him, too. That confirmed how serious this was. She had hoped he was going to tell her it would all be all right, that there was nothing to worry about.

"Ah, honey."

He'd read her like always. How did he do that so well?

He tugged her to him. Didn't even give her a choice. And that was okay. Being in his arms felt good and right, for this set of circumstances. She could stay there forever. Or at least for a very long time.

Until this was all over would be nice.

"I can't wait for this to be done. But I'm worried about Deputy Cosgrove. He wouldn't just leave me like that. What if he's not just some-where on that phone call and we got separated? What if he's dead?"

Griffin hadn't wanted to bring up that pos-sibility. "Don't even think like that. We'll find him, Alice. Don't worry." Why was he getting her hopes up? He wasn't sure exactly but maybe his words had been meant as much for himself as they were for Alice. In all honesty, he had a bad feeling about the deputy. He wanted to find the man alive and well somewhere, and yet, if that was the case, he had a few choice words to share with him for leaving her side.

She blew out a breath.

"Regardless if we find him or not, I'm here now," Griffin said. "I'm going to keep you safe. He's relieved of duty." The deputy wasn't going to be at his best or on full alert after a long night. So maybe he shouldn't be too hard on him.

"What? Am I suddenly your priority? And he's relieved on whose authority?"

He turned to her, shocked at the bitterness in her words.

She threw up her hands. "I'm sorry. I shouldn't have said that."

"No, it's okay. I deserved that. I should have stayed with you until this was over rather than heading out to join the raid. But I'm here now. So you're sticking with me. That is, unless you object. Oh, and it's on my uncle's, the sheriff's, authority. When he knew I was headed to Gideon, he asked me to help out. But I would be here, right here with you, even if he hadn't."

He studied her, gauged her reaction.

She shrugged, which disappointed him more than he would have thought possible.

"Of course I don't object. I'm glad you're here. But I don't want you to get hurt."

"How about we both stay alive." He grinned, trying to lighten the mood. "And get out of here for starters. We need to find the missing deputy and stay out of trouble. We can't stay here. We're like sitting ducks." He glanced out the windows. "Stick with me."

Before he moved to the second-floor apartment, the phone rang. Alice stared at it but didn't move.

"Aren't you going to answer that?"

"Probably just someone who wants to make reservations. Voice mail can get it."

"Could it be Cosgrove?"

Alice snatched up the phone. "Wilderness, Inc." She pressed Speakerphone.

"Alice, I'm so glad I got you. This is Tina from over at Ricky's. We found your deputy."

Griffin stepped forward as though he would

stop her next words in case they were too awful. "Where is he?" Griffin asked.

"Is he all right?" Alice leaned against the counter like she was bracing herself for the worst.

"Bubba found him on the floor in a storage closet."

"But is he all right, Tina?" Alice demanded. "Is he okay?"

"He's been stabbed, but he's alive. I think he was left for dead, but we found him in time. And what a mess of blood—"

"Tina!" Griffin cut her off.

"Oh, sorry. We sent him over to the clinic. He's alive and I think he's going to stay that way."

"Thanks for letting us know." Alice was about to hang up the phone—

"There's more. He…he had a message for you."

"Wait, he had a message?" Alice asked. "What message?"

"Just a second. I want to make sure I got it right." Background noise interrupted the line. Rustling paper erupted through the speaker.

Griffin grew frustrated with the waitress and her communication efforts. He wanted to march over to the clinic right now to find out what he needed to know from the deputy himself, but that could prove dangerous.

"What's the message?" he asked.

"Sorry." Her voice shook. "Bubba handed it over to me. He's too upset to talk to you."

"Can you please tell us what the deputy said?"

"Oh, it wasn't the deputy that said it. The message was written on a sheet of paper and… oh, how can I say this—" a sob broke through her voice "—the knife used to stab the deputy also secured the paper with the message."

FOURTEEN

Alice opened her mouth and covered it as if to hold back the scream that never came. Griffin reached for her, but she stepped away from him.

Griffin snatched up the phone and hit the speaker button, effectively turning that off. Alice tried to take the phone but he held her away.

"Griffin here. Tell me the message." Maybe he was a controlling jerk, and he was selfish more than anything. Selfish and weak. But he couldn't stand to see the look on Alice's face. He wouldn't let her hear the message. It would go through him first, and then he would be the one to break it to her, if he had to.

"Give me the phone!"

He turned to her then and scowled. "Wait, Alice. Just wait. Let me do this."

When she saw the anger and concern flashing in his gaze, she backed off. At least, he hoped that's what she'd seen. It was what he'd tried to convey.

"Now, Tina, I'm sorry you've had to go through this. I know this is difficult for you. But we're in a bit of a hurry here so could you please read me the note?"

Griffin kept his eyes locked on Alice's wide gaze.

Tina cleared her throat. "I'm coming for you. Run again and someone close to you will die."

Acid boiled in his gut. "Thank you," his voice croaked the words. It sounded like it came from outside his body down a long tunnel. Griffin hung up before she could say more. He didn't need to know anything else. Those brutal words confirmed all his fears.

"What?" Alice whispered. "What…what did the message say?"

"Nothing we didn't already know. He wants to get to you."

Griffin eyed the windows. Alice approached him until he couldn't avert his gaze.

"What else? He said something else, what was it?"

He didn't want to tell her. What good would that do?

"What did he say, Griffin?"

Pain clenched his heart and he shook his head.

"If you don't tell me, I'm just going to imagine the worst anyway."

A lump formed in his throat. "Okay. The message said if you run again, he'll kill someone close to you."

"Oh…" Alice pressed her face in her hands. She bent over at the waist.

She didn't know the worst of it. He'd called Cooper and left the man a message to get back to town. He'd detailed as much as he could. Cooper would likely call the rest of them back to town, and once they learned what Alice was up against, they'd come running. Until that moment when Griffin had called them, everyone truly close to Alice had been far away and safe, out of this man's reach. Griffin's heart ached as it splintered, shattered into pieces at what he'd done. The devastation that could happen. But how could he have known?

He thought Alice would buckle and he reached out, but he had no idea how to comfort her in this. Except for one thing. "He's not going to get to you. He'll have to go through me first."

She shot up, her face red. "See, that's what I *don't* want to happen. Don't you get it?" She averted her gaze and now she was the one to pace, her hand at her forehead. "What am I going to do? What am I going to do?"

He grabbed her wrist. "*We're* going to get out of here. *We*, do you understand?"

And somehow, he'd have to contact Cooper again and convince him to stay away. Like that would happen.

Her big blue eyes turned even darker as they stared at him. She looked caught in the headlights. Dazed. She shook her head. "No. You're not even supposed to be here."

Then he grabbed both wrists and pulled her against him. "This is exactly where I'm supposed to be. Get that through your head. I'm here for a reason and that reason is you."

She tried to pull away but he held tight. "Do you understand?"

Unshed tears along with fear pooled in her eyes but she nodded. He took her in his arms. Squeezed her close, nice and tight. "We're going to get through this together, Alice. Don't worry."

He released her and then crept up the stairs to the apartment. Slowly looked inside, Alice close behind. He peeked out the windows. The guy had tried to approach the apartment before. Griffin tried to decide on their best strategy. Should they wait it out here, in a relatively defensible location? But how long would they have to wait? Too much could go wrong.

And he couldn't possibly barricade all the

entrances. If they called others in town to help protect Alice, then someone would inevitably get hurt. Neither of them wanted that.

"We're not going to stay here, are we?" she asked. "I feel like we're trapped, Griffin. I don't want to be trapped. He could light a fire to this place. Months ago, someone burned the barbecue place. If we stay, he could burn us out." She shuddered.

He could tell it had seriously affected her. That was it then. Getting out and as far away from this wilderness as possible was the best plan.

He led her down the stairs again.

"What are you doing?"

"Just trying to decide on a safe exit." Glancing out the window between the miniblinds he could see the woods a few yards back from the building. They would be too vulnerable leaving the apartment from the back exit. Too vulnerable walking out the front door, also. "Come on."

Griffin moved to a side window. He tugged his weapon out and chambered a round. Held it at the ready as he looked out the window. Jammed his weapon back in the holster, then unlocked the window.

"Are you serious? We're going out the window?"

"We can sneak over to the next business and

make our way around to my motorcycle. Going out the obvious exits would be too…well, obvious."

"I don't know, Griffin. Seems to me if he's watching and waiting, he's going to see us leaving no matter what."

"Maybe. But this is our best option right now if we're going to leave." He slowly and quietly removed the screen. "I'll go first and make sure it's safe."

"Maybe I should go first. I don't think he wants to kill me yet, but he'll kill you if he realizes you're helping me escape."

Griffin glanced at her as he eased out the window, then hopped down. "Wait here."

Pressed against the wall, he made his way to the corner to peer around, his weapon positioned and ready to aim and fire to protect Alice.

Her last words kept repeating in his head. That's what Griffin wanted to understand. Why did the guy want her alive? Really? He'd wanted her taken alive back in the woods. Why not simply kill her? She was the witness who could nail him.

He must have some kind of grudge against her that went beyond that. The kind of grudge that meant he had plans for Alice. Horrible, brutal plans for her.

The only good thing in all of this was that Griffin had listened to his gut. At least he'd come back. He wasn't sure he could thank God enough that he'd responded to that sixth sense telling him he should return for her. He'd spent his adult life photographing and document-ing battles and natural disasters. Tragedy in every form, and it was almost like the worse the tragic scene, the better for the media, which sickened him. He wanted to do more than sim-ply document, even though his part was to ex-pose the evil in this world so that someone else could come in and fix it. But that didn't always happen.

And now he had a chance to make an actual difference. He could save a life. Not just any life. But Alice Wilde's life. He couldn't imagine a life he'd rather save more than hers.

He couldn't imagine his life without her. He chided himself for the thought.

If he wanted to concentrate, Griffin had to shove away the cruel thoughts of what the man would do to Alice if he got his hands on her. In this moment, he couldn't afford to let his at-tention slip. They were at their most vulnera-ble position right now, leaving the Wilderness, Inc. offices.

The man after her had to suspect they were inside and would come out at some point. As

Alice had said, he was probably watching the exits right now. If he was alone he couldn't be everywhere at once, which was to their advantage. But Griffin didn't know if the man was working alone in Gideon in his pursuit of Alice, and if he had left all his firepower back at his marijuana operation. Maybe the man believed that once he took out the deputy, Alice would have no one to call to help her.

But he hadn't counted on Griffin being there.

Griffin crept over to the back corner of the house and peeked around.

A fist filled his vision.

"Griffin!"

Alice had leaned out the window.

Someone punched him in the face, but he'd quickly regained his ground. A weapon fired off.

She climbed out, fell to the ground, got to her feet and ran to Griffin's aid.

God, please help us!

She had her own weapon drawn but with the two men using brute strength, their bodies entangled one second, then fighting it out with their fists the next, she feared shooting the wrong man.

"Stop it!" She fired her weapon into the ground. Surely that would get their attention.

They would disengage and she could point her gun at Bearded Man who'd come for her.

But nothing happened.

"Help, somebody help!" She gasped for breath. Hated seeing this man who obviously had skills attacking Griffin, though Griffin returned as good as he got. Maybe others would gather and help pull the men apart.

But then a young couple ran around the corner between the buildings. "What is it? What's happening?"

"No, get back!" Alice realized her mistake in calling for help. Someone could get hurt.

When she returned her attention to the fighting men, Bearded Man stood over Griffin, pointing his gun at his head. *Oh, Lord, please*…this can't be happening.

"No! Please, don't shoot him." Alice ran forward. She pointed her own weapon at the back of Bearded Man's head. "I'll kill you if you don't drop your weapon."

The man only laughed. He was laughing at her?

"Drop it now," she repeated.

Could she really do it? Could she shoot a man in the back? Never taking her aim from the man's head, she stepped around to the side so she could better see Griffin.

On the ground, he gasped for breath. Sweat

beaded on his forehead. Dirt smudged his face and clothes. Fear and regret lodged behind his eyes and in her soul. She read it in his gaze.

He was going to do something, but what?

Bearded Man spread his arms out, his elbows at ninety-degree angles. Wind rushed from her lungs in relief.

Her mistake. The man turned so fast she didn't have a chance and grabbed her weapon from her. Then he had her. He held the gun to her temple. "I'm just going to leave with her now," he said to Griffin. "Try anything and I'll kill her, then you. I'd prefer to take her alive."

Grief and anger boiled inside. She twisted in his grip. Tried to escape. Griffin looked on in horror. Then his expression grew hard as he climbed to his feet.

"Don't," the man ordered. "Just stay there. Stay down. You're nothing but a dog. Follow my commands." He spit the words out. "I have her now."

Griffin held his hands out. "Take me instead."

"I don't want you. I have special things planned for her. In fact…I have something special planned for you…" The man pulled the weapon away from her head and aimed at Griffin. Anticipating his next move, Alice twisted her body in his grasp hoping to throw his aim off, just as he fired the weapon.

But it was no use.

Griffin went down on his back.

"No!" she screamed and tried to pull away from him.

Run to Griffin.

But the man was stronger than she could have imagined. All that self-defense her brothers had taught her, all the muscle power gained from rowing on the river and wilderness training, and it couldn't match this man's strength. The man held her with an iron-tight grip and dragged her behind the buildings to who knew where.

She saw a few Gideonites gathering around Griffin, drawn by the sound of the gunshot. Some looking on in horror as she was abducted, but no one tried to interfere. They saw that this man dragging her had a gun.

"You killed him. You didn't have to kill him."

Alice didn't care what happened to her anymore. She just didn't care. She wanted her own vengeance against this man. Let him take her. She would wait for the right moment and take her own revenge. God would have to stand in her way, if He wanted the vengeance.

The man huffed while dragging her deadweight. And that's what she'd become. Weak and helpless. She never would have thought it. She heard a scuffle, a grunt and he dropped her. She fell to the ground. The man had released her. She got up to run but realized…

Griffin?

He grabbed her and ran behind a vehicle. Fired his weapon and received gunfire in return. Bearded Man ran behind more vehicles and disappeared.

She grabbed his face in her hands. "You're alive? But how? I saw him shoot you! I thought…"

He pulled his shirt open. "Vest. I had it on to go into the woods. Never took it off."

She ran her finger over the dent in the vest. "It has to hurt."

"Hurt more seeing him take you from me."

They both laughed a sob together. She pressed her forehead against his chest. He winced. She eased back. Closed her eyes. Tears slid from the corners. "It was like my worst nightmare, the dream I had last night, watching you get shot. I thought you were dead." She opened her eyes. "Don't ever do that to me again!"

"I'll do my best but I can't make any promises." He took her hand. "Let's get out of here. Now that the whole town is out in the street, and he's on the run, it's our chance to get away."

He tugged her along and she willingly followed, relief and gratitude surging through her veins.

God, thank You, thank You...

She felt more for this man than she could let herself admit. She couldn't afford to care about him, but she had lost all control when it came to her feelings for Griffin.

He approached his high-powered motorcycle, dragging her with him.

"Where are we going?"

"We're taking my Busa and getting out of Gideon. Getting as far from here as possible until this is over."

Alice nodded her agreement. Good idea. Griffin handed over an extra helmet. He climbed onto the machine and Alice got on behind him. She wrapped her arms around his waist and pressed against his leather jacket, feeling the body armor still intact beneath. And held on tight. He started the engine and revved it a few times.

Yeah. High-powered. He steered it out of Gideon faster than she would have liked. A crowd had gathered and cheered them on. Everyone seemed to understand they had survived and needed to escape. As he left Gideon proper, she squeezed him, tugging him back a little.

He turned his head sideways. "What is it?"

"Please don't drive too fast. I can participate in extreme sports, but motorcycles scare me." She yelled it all so he could hear.

He nodded, then revved the engine some more. Yelled over his shoulder. "Only one way to cure that."

And took off.

Alice screamed instinctively, but the rush of fear she was expecting never came. Maybe motorcycles didn't scare her as much as she thought. Or maybe that fear just didn't count for much in these circumstances. They were running for their lives, getting out of Gideon while a firestorm approached the huge marijuana operation in the woods, and a crazy man wanted to abduct her, torture her and then kill her. Would he find a way to follow them?

Alice glimpsed behind her.

A big-wheeled Ford truck was on their tail. Was it the man after her? She twisted to get a good look at the driver and her heart palpitated. Twisting back, she yelled at Griffin again.

"He's onto us. He's right behind us!"

FIFTEEN

Griffin watched the grill of the approaching truck in the mirror.

He went WOT—wide-open throttle—increasing the speed until he was going as fast as he dared. The bike rumbled beneath him, ripping up the road. Arms squeezed him until he couldn't breathe as screams erupted from Alice. Any other time, he might smile, but escaping this terror was no smiling matter.

Under normal circumstances, he wouldn't sweat it. An approaching truck like the one behind him couldn't catch his motorcycle which had top speeds of two hundred miles an hour. The problem was this stretch of treacherous mountain road was loaded with switchbacks. Add in a nervous passenger hanging on for dear life on the back, Griffin wasn't positive he could go fast enough to lose the truck. He'd have to do some fancy maneuvering. Alice's weight, though minimal, was enough to throw off his balance on the bends as well as slow them down.

But he had to try.

Approaching a twist in the road that disappeared around a ridge, leaving him blind to what lay ahead, he slowed the machine. The grill grew bigger in his mirror, but he couldn't take it too fast at the corner or they'd go flying off the cliff side. He had a feeling that could be the truck driver's intention. Of course, that would mean the guy wouldn't get Alice back alive, but maybe the man had enough with his games and had decided to give up the torture in exchange for certain death.

"Griffin! Slow down!"

I hear ya, Alice...

Answering her would distract him. He had to concentrate. But she was smart enough to know that. He focused on the road. The familiar feel of the powerful motorcycle beneath him, and the woman at his back, as he steered across the pavement, avoided the occasional rockslide or boulder, and sliced through the air.

They made the corner but crossed over the double yellow line. An oncoming car laid on the horn as it nearly swiped them. *Too close. Much too close!* He swerved quickly back into his own lane, and increased speed to put as much distance between them and the truck as he could while he had the chance. But he couldn't carve the road—lean hard and nearly horizontal on the curves—enough on the switchbacks with Alice. He couldn't ride nearly fast enough. Add to that, alone he wouldn't care so much what might be around the next turn blocked from his view by the mountain, but Alice was his to protect from both the danger of a high-speed motorcycle ride and their pursuer who was closing in on them.

Even on his Busa, Griffin was hard-pressed to win this fight.

The truck's grill appeared in the mirror again. Though the driver had lost ground, he increased speed, his determination equal to Griffin's. Alice repositioned her arms and shifted on the seat behind him. She had to be terrified.

Approaching another switchback, he downshifted and braked to slow a little, but not too much or the truck would catch up with them. This was an impossible situation.

"Hold on!" he called over his shoulder.

He kept the speed faster than he would normally go with a passenger on a turn like this. Leaned to the right as they turned with the switchback, then sat upright again as the road straightened out. He leaned forward and Alice did the same. Speed was all about aerodynamics. As much as he loved riding this particular motorcycle, he never imagined he would be using it like this—to escape a killer—and with a woman he cared deeply about on the back, her life in as much danger from the killer as from this reckless, explosive motorcycle ride.

"Griffin, hurry. Faster." Alice's raised voice sounded desperate.

Faster? Alice wanted faster? They must be in real trouble. He glanced in the mirror. The truck sped around the corner, flying into the opposite lane as he made the twist in the road, and then onto the rocky ledge, barely avoiding running right off the side of the mountain. But then he swerved back onto the road and into the right lane as he gained traction and closed the distance.

Lord, how am I going to get us out of this? Help us! Help me to save Alice.

He punched it. They were going to die one way or another if he didn't come up with another plan. On an incline, the bike slowed, but so did the truck. Griffin gave it all he had, and would burn the engine up if necessary to increase speed on this steep hill.

He loved this motorcycle. But he was going to have to lose it in order to survive. If they kept going like this, they were going to wipe out. And that would be the absolute worst thing to happen on a bike at this speed.

Death by truck ramming.

Death by motorcycle crash.

Death either way. Take your pick.

He whipped around the corner at breakneck speeds, then found what he was looking for.

The perfect place to crash and die.

Alice kept her eyes squeezed shut. Every few seconds, though, she glanced behind them just to make sure she wasn't about to be smashed by that truck. The motorcycle's engine roared in her ears despite the helmet, vibrating through her core, but the truck behind them blasted out an intimidating sound of its own generated by headers and straight pipes. She wasn't sure which she was more afraid of—the truck behind them or the ride of her life on this motorcycle with crazy adrenaline junkie Griffin at the helm.

They took a corner much too fast and Alice thought she would lose the meager contents of her stomach. This was like the worst roller coaster ride she'd ever experienced. She couldn't shake the sense of imminent death.

Then suddenly the motorcycle slowed abruptly, and Griffin shouted.

"Hold on!"

"What do you think I've been doing?"

"Tighter, even tighter."

What is he doing? She had to be brave. She had to risk a look, and opened her eyes. He was headed for the trees.

He was going to crash them on purpose?

"What are you doing?" she yelled. Would he hear her in time? She absolutely didn't want to die. Not like this.

*Oh, God, Oh, God, Oh, God...*she cried out to Him as the bike bumped along and she could barely hold on to Griffin.

And then she fell off, her helmet smashing into a boulder, her body into the soft earth. She groaned and rolled to the side.

Gasped. "Griffin?"

Opened her eyes to see him standing next to his motorcycle through the trees and bushes. He appeared to fiddle with the throttle, then sent the machine off through the woods to crash, spectacularly.

"Oh. My—"

He ran back to her, a limp in his step. Knelt down. "We have to go!"

He snatched her up, running down the hill in the opposite direction from the motorcycle. "Are you okay?" he asked but kept on running, leading her through the trees toward the Rogue River as it entered a canyon.

Her body ached and trembled. "No, I'm not

okay. Thanks for asking. I see you didn't come away unscathed, either."

"Just a sprain." But Griffin didn't slow down. "We have to get away. Get out of here. Let him think we crashed back there."

She nodded. "Good thinking, I guess. But that's not going to fool him for long and now we're trapped between the mountain and the river without any transport."

"That's okay. It'll take him some time to figure that out. In the meantime, we're pushing farther away and hiding. As long as he doesn't know where we are and can't find us, we're better off doing this than we were on that mad race on the mountain road."

He crept dangerously close to a ledge as he pushed around a boulder. On the other side a flat, granite terrace overlooked the rushing river. Griffin eased down, and pulled her down to sit next to him. She took a moment to catch her breath, as did he.

God, when is this going to end?

"I'm sorry about that," he said.

"Which *that* are you talking about, exactly?"

He chuckled. "Back there. I'm sorry you fell off. I didn't mean for that to happen. I meant for us to get off the bike together."

She rubbed her backside. "I just have some bruises, is all. I'll live."

He tugged her helmet off. "And a cracked helmet. This won't do anyone any good like this. But it likely saved your life."

Alice pulled her knees up to her chin and pressed her forehead against her arms. She released a long, heavy sigh. "What next? We can't stay here. He's bound to catch up. Maybe we can ambush him this time, and just take him out."

She turned her head to study him.

His eyes had a wildness to them that scared her. "You'd want me to do that?"

"Sure, I would. If we don't capture him or take him out, then I'll have to look over my shoulder constantly for the rest of my life. I'll have to worry he'll go after someone close to me. We have to end this somehow."

He reached over and rubbed his thumb over her chin. "We had a brush with him already and that almost ended in the worst possible way."

"Let's keep going, then. We can hike upstream and find a place to call for help." Though she wasn't sure who exactly they'd call at the moment. Emergency calls out here were fielded at the county sheriff's department and they were occupied at the moment. Besides, even if they weren't occupied, no one could reach them in time.

Alice stood and led the way, following the

river's course, only upstream. Hiking downstream and they'd run into the canyon which they couldn't climb without equipment. Besides, Alice didn't have the energy left to tackle climbing in a canyon.

"I think our immediate goal is to get out of the area," Griffin said. "To get far away from here and lose this guy."

"Sure, you say that now that we lost our ride. And that was your call. You didn't ask me for my input."

He gestured ahead from where voices drifted. "I have an idea."

Just ahead on a small bank, several tents flapped in the wind. A family, and two couples, breaking camp.

"Oh yeah, what's that?" But she thought she could guess.

Alice glanced behind them up into the cliffs and woods. She hoped they weren't leading Bearded Man to these innocent people.

Up at the top of the cliff where they'd lingered, a dark-haired man stood looking through binoculars pointed directly at them. Alice's pulse jumped.

SIXTEEN

Time was up.

Griffin approached a man—the father, it appeared, of the three strapping teenage boys. His wife acted wary at their approach. Their eyes darted to the weapons in holsters both Alice and Griffin carried.

"Listen, we're in a bit of a bad situation," Griffin offered. He had to persuade them. "It's an emergency and we need your help."

The father glanced at his boys, then back to Griffin. "How can we help?"

"We need to borrow your raft," Alice blurted out.

"What?" The woman gasped. "No, you can't have our raft. Are you crazy? What are we supposed to use?"

Other campers had paused to watch. Two men from the next camp over eyed him. He couldn't afford to get in an argument, especially if it turned physical. "Look, I can pay you for your trouble, okay?"

The guy arched a brow.

"Forget it. We don't want your money," the woman said. "And you can't have our raft."

"We can take you with us. We'll take you where you need to go, right, Dad?" One of the sons spoke up, probably out of turn given the look his mother gave him.

"Just what kind of emergency is this?" his father asked.

"The kind of emergency you want no part of," Griffin said. "Someone…someone's trying to kill us, and we need to escape."

"So you're just going to leave us here to face them?" The woman started marching around, pacing in circles. "Tom, get them out of here. Make them leave. Now."

Griffin ignored her and drew closer to the man, lowering his voice. "We don't want any trouble or to bring harm to you or your family. In fact, we're trying to lead the trouble away. We need to escape. Please, just let us buy your raft."

"I don't know, maybe you're in trouble with the law. If you're fugitives then we need to keep you here."

Griffin didn't want to resort to pulling a weapon out and using it to force his way on the raft. For all he knew this man, the others on the beach, also carried for their protection. A shoot-out with these people was the last thing he wanted. Instead Griffin pulled his wallet out and showed his credentials to the man. "My name is Griffin Slater and I was a navy combat photographer. This is Alice Wilde and her family runs the Wilderness, Inc. Ever heard of that?"

"Oh yeah." The sons nodded.

"And here's four hundred bucks. I know it's not a fourth of what that raft cost you but it's all I have on me."

"Wow," the youngest son said. "You carry that much money in your wallet?"

Griffin nodded. "And not a penny more. For emergencies. You never know when you're going to need to buy a raft off someone."

The mother still appeared incredulous.

"You can call up the sheriff's department if you like and ask if we're legitimate. In fact, do me a favor and when you get a signal, call them just to let them know Griffin and Alice are in trouble and running from a bad guy. Tell them we've taken to the river."

The father appeared convinced and gestured to the raft. "Take it and keep your money."

Griffin nodded. "Thanks. And if I can, I'll

let you know where I left it. What's your name and contact information?"

"Kendall. Tom Kendall." The man pulled out a business card and handed it over to Griffin.

"Well, Tom, maybe you and your family can hitch a ride with these other guys."

"Sure thing," another man offered. "We'll get them down the river."

The woman pursed her lips and shook her head, glaring at her husband, clearly unhappy with his decision.

Griffin wasn't sure he blamed her. After all, they were leaving a family here. Alice stepped up to her. "If you guys don't want to take the rafts, you can hike back up that way to another lodge. It's slower, but it's safe."

"Oh yeah? Why don't you guys do that instead of taking our raft?"

Alice peered at Griffin and arched a brow. "Because like I said, it's slower. We need to make a speedy getaway."

"Fair enough," Tom said. He glanced at something behind them. "And I'd say you'd better get going."

"I appreciate your help."

Tom handed off two life jackets.

Alice and Griffin secured the jackets, and she offered an apologetic look to the family. Griffin hopped into the raft and offered his hand to Alice. Though she didn't need any assistance, she took it and then jumped into the raft and grabbed the oars. Between the two of them, they quickly urged the boat out into the middle of the river.

"I don't like this," she said. "I don't like leaving them stranded there. What if he finds them and hurts them? Remember his warning?"

"It's too late now. What choice did we have? No matter what, they stand between us and him. At least he'll see us in the raft and will know we're getting away. If he wants to stay on our trail, he can't avoid to waste time punishing the people who helped us."

They entered the canyon and both he and Alice glanced up at the cliffs, wary of being shot considering the last time they'd been in these waters. The river twisted in the canyon so they couldn't see too far behind them or in front of them.

A rapid-fire automatic weapon went off somewhere behind them, echoing through the gorge.

Alice and Griffin shared a look. What could that familiar, dreadful sound mean? Fear corded her throat and tightened.

"Griffin, we have to go back! We have to

check on them!" Alice started paddling against the current.

He moved over to her and grabbed her wrists. "No. That's not going to help them or us. You don't know what happened. You don't know if it has anything to do with those people we left behind."

"Are you insane? Of course it does. We need to get back to them. I'm going to give myself up."

Brutal anger flashed in his gaze. "If you think for one minute I'm going to let you do that, you're the one who's crazy. Now, give me those oars."

His gaze shifted to something behind them, something unspeakable behind his eyes. "Let's. Get. Moving!"

"I'll man the oars," she said, refusing to move but she slowly twisted to see what had caused Griffin's reaction. Another boat had entered the canyon behind them. Bearded Man was steering it by himself.

Her body shuddered. She wanted to slump over into the water and die. "Oh, God, please, let them be okay."

This was torture, pure torture.

Please, can this be over. Until it was over, anyone she came in contact with was in danger.

She thought of Deputy Cosgrove. The Kendall family.

She would never feel free to walk in the woods again, if she survived this.

"Griffin?"

"Yeah?" His strained answer came between breaths as he paddled.

Though she was in great condition, the work they were putting into this had her breathing hard, too. It was a matter of life and death. If Bearded Man got too close, it was conceivable that he could shoot them. The last thing they needed was to get into a gun battle on these rafts in the river. They could all end up drowned.

"I'm thinking about what's ahead of us." Her muscles starting to scream, she sucked in another breath. "Rainie Falls and then…"

"Blossom Bar. Don't be afraid, Alice. You can do this. We'll be fine. You're the best, remember?"

Alice glanced over her shoulder. The man following them fell behind. Hope infused her that they could lose him, they could do this. Except even if they escaped him, this would never end. "I'm not scared about Rainie Falls or the Bar." Rainie was rated a Class V and Blossom Bar was only a Class IV. "In fact, I think we should use that to our advantage. This time, I *want* to lose someone in the rapids. If Rainie Falls doesn't get him, then maybe the Picket Fence will." Adding him to the number of others.

Had she really just said that? *God, help me, am I wrong to think this way?*

"Alice, you sure about this?"

"I'm not sure it really matters. He's following us. There's only one way down the river. I'm not going to help him. There's no way I safely can."

She glanced over her shoulder. Rowing the paddles, Griffin nodded. "I see your point."

A smattering of other rafting enthusiasts shared the river with them, including two kids in kayaks. Alice didn't want these innocent people to become collateral damage.

"Except, this time, instead of shooting for the right side of the rapids, we're going to purposefully shoot for the left."

"Explain."

"Between the two of us, we know to avoid the Picket Fence. Unless he's been on the river he wouldn't know. He can only follow us. And only those especially skilled can take that side without getting dumped."

"What if he's trained?" Griffin asked. "What if he has the skills? There's a chance that this isn't going to buy us anything except risking our own lives."

Point taken. She didn't respond other than to say, "Rainie Falls coming up, so let's focus."

On the other side of the falls, they floated and caught their breath while watching the man who followed them.

"Come on, Alice, we have to keep putting distance between us. We can't stop to watch him."

Still, Alice positioned herself with the oars so she could watch the man. Her hopes faded. He handled Rainie Falls like a pro.

SEVENTEEN

Fear and disappointment filled Alice. She paddled harder, working with the current of the river to gain speed. Her pursuer seemed to stare right through her, even from this distance, and a wicked grin spread across his face. That he was close enough she could see his grin infused her with renewed terror.

"He's no novice," she mumbled to herself.

"I see that."

She glanced at the groups of people who made it over Rainie Falls, some of whom now set up their camps near Whiskey Creek to spend the afternoon exploring the region. They could expect to see more campers along the next few miles of the river. How did they escape this crazy man without anyone getting hurt?

"Should we get out at the next possible place?" Griffin asked.

"You mean Rogue River Ranch?"

"I have no clue what it's called. Just the next stop."

"No." Alice's answer came surprisingly quick. "I want to face off with him in this river. Try to lose him this way."

"Whatever you say." Doubt edged Griffin's tone.

"Maybe I'm crazy, but I don't know what else to do. I don't want others to get in the middle and get hurt. If I have to face him anyway, I'd prefer that happens in this river, where I'm strongest." Could she really hope to end this in the river? *Maybe I am crazy.* This wasn't a competition for a medal. Someone pursued her with deadly weapons and if he couldn't take her alive, he would kill her. She resolved that she would die rather than let him take her.

"Glad to hear you got your confidence back," he said.

It was more one-part confidence, two-parts no better options. "We'll just keep going and see what happens."

She paddled harder. Floating down the river like this with a man bent on killing her less than a quarter mile from her, always in view, was surreal. There wasn't any other word for it. This ordeal would reduce her to her basest survival instincts before it was all over. All she could think about was being out of the water and safe and…in Griffin's arms.

She had to shake that image, the desire and need in her.

"What's next, Alice?"

"Mule Creek Canyon comes after the Rogue River Ranch. You'll see the sandy beaches and lots of people there."

"We went through that canyon before with the sheriff, right?"

"Yep. It had the vertical rocks on both sides. Canyon is half a mile long. Weird currents in there so we'll need to focus. Use our skills to keep from slamming into the walls. Okay?"

"I think rapids met us at the entrance, right?"

"Oh yeah. Those rapids are called 'Jaws' for a reason. And after the canyon we'll hit Blossom Bar." All of this she knew with her eyes closed. Knew by her terrified heart. The biggest drop on the river would always be seared in her memory, especially since the day someone drowned on her watch.

"Breathe, Alice. Just breathe. Don't let him intimidate you."

"Yeah, right. He's bearing down on us. I'm starting to question our decision to take the river."

"No time, no point in second-guessing. We

made our decision with the choices presented to us."

He was only trying to encourage her, but he was entirely too positive to be credible. Steady and slow, she took his advice and breathed in deeply.

The canyon was upon them much too fast.

"So this is it, Griffin. The next mile or so we need to somehow lose him. Dunk him in the water and make our escape. And hope the river keeps him forever." Though it seemed kind of cruel. "It seems so weird. This place is usually a fun rafting trip for families, and now this man has turned it into a living terror."

Griffin reached over and squeezed her shoulder. "We're in this together, Alice. We'll make it out. Don't worry."

She wanted to soak in his reassurance and believe him. Believe that he was in it with her. But it was so hard to completely trust the man. Still, after everything they'd been through together, she knew she could trust him to protect her, trust him with her life. It was more her heart that she worried about. And he'd come back this time, which shook up her resolve, overrode the cautioning of her good sense not to fall for him. Was there more to it than he sensed she was in danger?

She shrugged off the ridiculous thoughts

tugging her emotions in every direction and focused back on their predicament. The man chasing them gained on them thanks to a fast-moving current and she caught sight of the automatic weapon propped in his raft. Her mouth went dry.

"I guess you see he's gained on us."

"Yep. I see him." Griffin had lost his reassuring tone. "What can we do?"

"Keep paddling. Keep praying," she said. Her instructions sounded pathetic and feeble. "Then get ready for Jaws, the first drop into Mule Creek Canyon."

Water caught their vessel and tossed it from side to side, splashed into the raft, soaking them. Alice shouted instructions to Griffin. They had to keep from being dashed against the canyon walls in the insane currents. And in turn, her muscles shouted at her, screaming with exertion. But...finally...they made it through Jaws. Avoided the spots where the water boiled.

"Hold on. Another Class II coming up." She caught her breath. Rested her arms for half a minute. "You'll love this one. It's called Coffee Pot."

He chuckled behind her, though with a killer closing in on them, it wasn't really a laughing matter. "Who was the person to name these?

You can pretty much guess how the names came about."

"Yeah. Coffee Pot is hot and caffeinated."

Another rapid behind them, she never took her eyes off their assailant. "Any other time, we could stop and admire Stair Creek. Those waterfalls."

"Yeah, I remember them. But you didn't give us an official tour before."

"No time then. No time now."

Kayakers had paused in the eddy to admire the falls. Alice feared warning them would only draw the danger to them. Too many people on the river. And today, they couldn't know just how much danger they were in.

All because Alice and Griffin had this bright idea.

Oh, God, please let us lead this man far away from others. Please don't let anyone get hurt. I would never wish anyone's death, but I ask for your help in getting free of this stalker. For justice to somehow prevail in all of this.

And for us to survive, come out of it unscathed. But was that really an option anymore? Alice's life had already been changed forever.

Salty tears streamed down her cheeks, surprising her.

"You okay?" Griffin asked.

"Yeah, I'll be fine."

"Isn't our big drop coming up?"

"Yep." Alice glared at the man closing in on them in a raft of his own. Could he see the anger pouring from her gaze? Because now anger had just about replaced her fear.

But her thoughts had been misplaced as he pulled out the automatic weapon and fired multiple earsplitting rounds off into the air. Alice ducked, a purely reflexive move, but if he decided to shoot at her, she and Griffin would have to fire back. Screams erupted and echoed throughout the canyon as tourists both in rafts and along the cliffs above took cover. A tourist group scouted the rapids instead of floating, walking along the cliffs to the right. They disappeared out of sight. She hoped no one up there had been shot when he'd aimed his weapon upward.

What was wrong with him? It looked like he was growing tired of chasing her, and wasn't thinking clearly. Was he starting to make mistakes, this the first step in his ultimate failure? She had reason to hope and yet, she was terrified his mistakes would cost more lives.

"You idiot! Stop it! Just stop it!" she yelled at him. "You're going to kill innocent people."

She had no idea if he heard her. Maybe he did because he spewed obscenities in reply and unfortunately she could make him out just fine. And then realization dawned.

"Griffin…" Her heart palpitated. Alice closed her eyes, dizziness sweeping over her. She absolutely could not afford to lose it now. Not here.

Griffin gripped her shoulders. "Easy now, take it easy."

"I'm okay. I'm okay." She sucked in a breath. "I…I remember why his face is familiar. I saw him before at the funeral."

"Funeral? What funeral? Who is he?" Griffin kept a grip on Alice. She shuddered.

He watched the man after them, steadily closing the distance.

When Alice still didn't answer, he shook her. She stared at him in a daze.

"Alice, who is he?"

She blew out a breath. Water rushed around them, drawing them closer to the next round of rapids. Griffin waited patiently, but they had to focus on Blossom Bar coming up next. He could hear the roar of the twisting, boiling water already.

Finally, she responded. "He's… Steve Hanover's father."

The name sounded familiar to Griffin, but he couldn't place it. "And who is Steve Hanover?"

"Steve is the man who drowned on my guided tour of the river."

Her words punched him in the gut.

Oh. No. That wasn't good. Not good at all. *Of course*, she would have to remember just as they approached Blossom Bar, the very place where it happened. That had been what it took for her to recall—staring at the man's father as they faced the Picket Fence. Their pursuer's tenacity made more sense now. It wasn't just that she'd stumbled on his marijuana operation that was even now likely being destroyed. The man also blamed Alice for his son's death. Maybe that alone hadn't been enough to push him over the edge, but her discovery of his illegal operation had certainly been the trigger to set him after her.

Griffin shifted forward. "Here, change places with me."

"Why? I'm in the right position to guide us through."

"I want to protect you if he shoots."

"No offense, Griffin, but your protection won't do us any good if we get dunked. Let me be the guide here. I'd say you could ride right there facing me except that would throw off our balance now that I have the feel of this raft."

He frowned. She was stubborn, but probably right.

"Now it all makes sense. That's why he didn't kill me." Her face paled.

Griffin wouldn't voice what they both had already realized—the man wanted her alive because this was personal to him. She'd cost him not only his son, but also millions of dollars by leading the law to his illegal marijuana operation.

"You should get back into position," she said. "We only get one shot at this."

With no time to think about the attacker closing in on them, Griffin followed Alice's instructions, guiding the raft over the boiling rapids as it tumbled over and over. Matching her strokes. Forward, back paddle, draw and pry. Until they'd pushed beyond the danger. But even then, his tension remained high.

"We made it, Griffin. We made it!"

Griffin held his breath, watching the man behind them navigate. Griffin's hope soared when the man almost went up on the Picket Fence of boulders, and his raft came close to flipping. But he made it through them, too.

And Griffin couldn't look at Alice, couldn't stand to see the disappointment and fear.

He had to do something. Get them out of this. His idea to take the river hadn't worked to save them. Tugging his firearm out of the holster, Griffin looked around. Did he have any options? Choices that didn't call for a gun battle here in these rafts on the river? They couldn't keep going like this indefinitely. The man was wearing them down. Someone would make a mistake.

A shot rang out. Blinding pain stabbed him.

EIGHTEEN

"Griffin!" Alice screamed.

He tumbled over the raft's edge and into the river.

And her world turned upside down. Fear got a choke hold on her and she couldn't breathe. But if she didn't move, Griffin could die.

Hunkering low, she bent over the side of the raft and waited for him to come back up, hoping he would reach for her and she would grab him.

Come on, come on. Her heart hammered as terror gripped her, the ache of potential loss crippled her. When he didn't resurface, she gained control over the fear paralyzing her. One quick glance behind her at the man who fired off the shot. Would he shoot her, too?

She couldn't let that happen but more important, Griffin needed her. She gulped a breath, then dived into the swirling water. The current snatched her up and tugged her deep even though she wore a life vest. Her eyes burned in the cool water as she searched for him.

I can't lose you, Griffin. Not like this...

Not because he'd been shot by a man after her, or because he drowned when she could have saved him. Better that he left her behind never to see her again. That he walked away from her of his own accord to live a long life far away from her instead of being taken by an untimely death. *Please, God, let it be so. Let him live to see another day. To get the chance to leave this place. And I'll let go of the pain and hurt this time. I'll let go of him.*

No regrets. No resentment.

Alice's lungs burned, and she hadn't yet caught sight of the one man she'd ever fallen for. She couldn't let this river take someone else from her. She breached the surface, sucked in air as the river's flow swept her away from her raft. Twenty-five yards from her she spotted a man floating facedown.

Her gut spasmed.

No. Oh no! "Griffin, I'm coming. Hang in there." She refused to let the fear trembling through her limbs keep her from him.

Alice thrust forward, swimming with the current to catch him. He disappeared from view for a moment, and then she caught sight of him again. Reaching Griffin, she tugged him over on his back. Blood drenched his shoulder, his lips were blue and he wasn't breathing. Her gaze flicked to the killer after her. If she went to shore to perform CPR, he'd catch up to her. She would save Griffin, but she couldn't escape their pursuer. Still, she knew what had to be done.

Securing an arm around him, she swam him toward the bank, pulling him along with her. The raft drifted ahead of them, too far away and moving too rapidly for her to catch. Her muscles burned as she swam with all her strength. Maybe… Just maybe… If they could reach the riverbank they'd have a chance. She could revive Griffin and they could run or they could hide. Somehow find safety. Find someone who could help them survive this.

But deep inside, she knew she was reaching for the impossible. And admitting that, Alice faced the truth head-on. She was beginning to think she wouldn't survive this. But there might still be a chance for Griffin to live.

Come on, come on, come on…

Near the riverbank her feet touched sand and rocks. Grabbing his arms, she lugged Griffin toward the gray sand of the beach until finally she released him. She began preparing to do CPR. Get him breathing again if it wasn't already too late.

But the simple action of tugging his arms forced water from his lungs. Though he coughed up water and was breathing on his own, he was out cold. She rolled him over as water continued from his lungs. When he groaned she hoped he would wake up but he didn't. Now that he breathed, she examined the shoulder area saturated with blood—shot in a place where the body armor hadn't protected him. Alice quickly tore a strip from his sleeve and wrapped it tightly over his shoulder and around his back to help stem the bleeding. But if he remained unconscious and wouldn't wake up, it didn't much matter. They couldn't flee.

In her peripheral vision she spotted the raft carrying her pursuer growing closer. He could take aim and shoot her right here and now if he wanted. She knew that. But she wouldn't leave Griffin to be finished off.

"Come on, Griffin. Please wake up."

She glanced around them, looking for an escape and realization dawned. Rock walls trapped this small cove, and in effect trapped them, too. Even if Griffin were to wake up, she doubted he could climb the walls with his new injury.

"It's no use," Hanover called from the river. "You can't escape me. I won't let you get away from me again."

Think, Alice. You have to think. What could she use as her weapon? She'd lost hers in the river. But Griffin had one.

She found his holster. Empty. He must have taken it out just in case and then dropped it when he was shot.

She turned to face her pursuer as he guided the raft up and onto the riverbank. He hopped off and secured it. Alice backed away from him, luring him from Griffin in case he thought to hurt the man when he was down. Kill him. She wouldn't put it past him.

"What do you want from me?"

He strolled toward her, kicking up pebbles and sand as he cornered her. "I think you already know."

She shook her head, dread cording around her throat. Tightening. Choking her.

Another group of rafters passed them in the river. No one even glanced their direction. She didn't want to bring harm to others but she was desperate.

"Help! Someone please help!" she called out to the passersby.

But her cries for help weren't heard over the rush of the river. Hanover turned to look at the other rafters, lifting his sidearm—not the AR-15 rifle, this time—as if he were prepared to take them all on if they tried to help. Alice rushed him in that instant. Twisted her leg behind his. He dropped to the sand but brought her down with him, his hands gripping her wrists. Despite her strength and agility, he was much too strong for her.

Still, she'd disarmed him.

His weapon lay a few feet away. She fought against him. If she could free herself for even a second, she could reach the weapon before him. He smacked her away from him, knocking her in the wrong direction. Alice hit the ground hard. The coppery taste of blood filled her mouth.

Her head spinning, she swiped at the blood trickling from her lips and refocused on Hanover. She had to stop him.

But it was too late. He already gripped the gun in his hands. Pointed it at her.

And fired.

The gunshot echoed in the small canyon. Alice instinctively flinched. Squeezed her eyes and waited for the pain that accompanied the bullet.

Am I shot?

A few seconds passed and she finally drew in a breath. Opened her eyes and glanced down. Ran her hands over her uninjured midsection. Then glanced up as the man marched toward her.

He'd fired a warning shot.

The first time she'd faced this man, she'd been terrified, but she'd had a weapon then, and she'd had the woods in which to run and escape. Here and now, she was all too aware of the terrain that kept them trapped in the small alcove along the Rogue River. She couldn't have picked a worse place to bring Griffin ashore, but she'd needed to revive him. She'd had no choice if she wanted him to live.

Before Hanover reached her, she stood and backed away. He closed the distance, fire raging behind his dark gaze.

"I see in your eyes you remember me. You know who I am."

She slowly nodded. "I saw you at Steve's funeral. You're…you're his father. I'm so sorry about what happened. But he knew the risks. Everyone who gets on the river knows the risks."

"So you don't think you're responsible."

Hadn't she held herself responsible for these last eight months? "I blamed myself all this time, but the truth is I did the best I could and I was as careful as it's possible to be. Things happen sometimes. I know that can't change the fact that he died. And I'm so sorry for your loss."

He nodded as though he accepted her condolences. "I wanted to see you pay even then, but I couldn't risk doing anything that might draw attention to me and to my *business* out here in the wilderness. And then you showed up at my very lucrative operation, and because of that, because you reported what you saw, I'll lose millions of dollars. If being the one I hold responsible for my son's death wasn't enough, you have destroyed me *twice* now!" He'd worked himself into a fury, spittle erupting from his mouth as he got in her face and yelled.

Then he pressed the cold barrel of his weapon under her chin. "And do you know what happens now?"

"No…" Her trembling reply sounded foreign to her ears. This wasn't who she was. She was stronger than this. And if she wasn't, then it was time she started.

"You belong to me now. I'm going to take you and you'll belong to me, whatever I come up with until I grow bored."

"You're sick, you know that? It's not my fault you chose to grow your weed on public lands where anyone could find it."

"No. Not anyone. Just you, Alice Wilde— wilderness guide extraordinaire."

The man grabbed her arm. Alice punched him in the nose. But he returned the favor, slapping her hard across the face again. The force of his action jarred her, knocking her to the ground again. Her cheek stung the first time, but this time had gone numb, though her teeth ached. But Alice didn't give him the satisfaction of groaning in pain. Instead, she stared at him, unwilling to show him her fear.

He jammed the gun into the back of her head. "You want to die now, that can be arranged. Or maybe I can simply hurt you, incapacitate you so you can't fight back. That way you suffer more."

You want to die now, that can be arranged. The deadly words drifted into his subconscious and jolted Griffin. Warning signals resounded in his head.

His mind grappled with the words.

No...stop...don't shoot her!

His body wouldn't respond. He sensed the man had Alice and was dragging her away from Griffin. Forever. He was taking Alice away to hurt her and then kill her. Griffin struggled to force his body to function, to respond...but it was like he was stuck in a dream and couldn't wake up. Slowly, he pulled himself from his unconscious state, from the dream, and shook off his stupor. He pressed his hands and knees into the sand and angled his head toward the river.

The man had forced Alice onto his raft and already steered out of the small eddy heading into the current. Griffin didn't have a chance of catching them if he didn't act now before swift water snatched the raft out of his reach.

And he'd better slip into the water before Hanover turned around and spotted him. He'd shoot to kill, and this time, he wouldn't miss. Griffin had to wonder at the Providence that had kept him alive to begin with. Hanover must have thought him dead or dying. Not worth the effort to check when he had to keep a close watch on Alice.

Crawling, he made his way to the river and continued forward until he could slip into the water. He relieved himself of the life vest. Under these circumstances, it would only get him killed. The coldness of the water bit through his injured shoulder and almost caused him to release the breath he held. But he had to ignore the gouging pain if he wanted to save Alice.

Please, God. Please let me save Alice.

With every stroke in the water, his wound ached, his arm barely responding to his efforts until finally the pain faded into numbness. Griffin focused on one thing only.

Alice.

He could make out the bottom of the raft and

would have to swim much faster if he wanted to catch up. He peeked above the surface and dragged in another breath. Alice locked gazes with him. The man had positioned her to do all the work as he pointed the weapon at her just below the edge of the raft so he wouldn't draw the attention of others on the river.

When she spotted Griffin, her eyes widened. And then she brought the oar up and around and slammed Hanover with it.

What was she doing? Putting herself in harm's way to give Griffin a chance. That's what.

He used the opportunity she'd give him. *God, please don't let him hurt her! Let me make it!*

Swimming hard and fast, he didn't even want to think about the suffering Alice must be experiencing at the hands of this purely evil person. Her screams reached his ears underwater just as he made the raft. He wasn't sure how he could crawl over the edge with his depleted energy and gunshot wound.

But maybe he didn't have to.

He held on and hefted himself halfway. That drew the man's attention off Alice who fought him with the oar. Hanover leaned closer and pointed his weapon point-blank at Griffin. Alice knocked it away with her oar. The man cried out in pain, and Griffin lunged forward, grabbed Hanover's arms and pulled him over the raft into the river with him.

The current caught them, but Griffin didn't let go. He prayed for enough strength to overpower this man. They bobbed along in the river, the man trying to loosen Griffin's grip on him. Neither of them wore life jackets.

"I'm going to stop you from hurting Alice. From ever getting your hands on her again." He ground out, letting his pent-up fury and adrenaline power him through.

"I'm going to kill you!" Hanover said.

"I don't care, as long as Alice is safe and I stop you from coming near her again."

The river towed the man under, but Griffin didn't let go as the man fought him. He returned the punches even as he gripped him in the most painful battle he'd experienced yet. His sudden burst of strength was quickly fading. If he didn't do something now, he was going to die. But he was all right with that if he took this man with him.

Griffin took in a long breath, then shoved them both deep, dragging the man under and deeper with him. Fate would decide which of them could hold his breath longer.

NINETEEN

Alice let the river carry the raft as she leaned over the edge, watching. The two men's heads had bobbed up and down in the water as they fought, but now they were gone. Just gone.

How did Griffin have the strength to even battle the man considering his gunshot wound? But being ex-military, he'd been trained how to push forward in the worst of circumstances, trained to overcome impossible odds.

Where she'd almost given up, lost hope, he had continued his efforts to try to triumph over evil. This time it wasn't to expose the wrong-doing through the lens of his camera, from a distance. This battle for good over evil, for life over death, was physical.

"Griffin!" *Oh, please, please be okay.*

The river carried the raft forward, oblivious to the fact two men had gone under.

"Oh, God, I can't lose Griffin in this river. Please…" She whispered on a sob. Alice scrambled around to the other side. "Griffin. Where are you?"

"Here," a voice said. "I'm here."

She jerked around. He barely hung on to the raft. Alice rushed to the side, reaching for him. She gripped his arms, and assisted him over and into the raft with her. Leaning against her, he dripped water on her and soaked her clothes as he gasped for breath.

Alice wrapped her arms around him. "I thought you were dead. I thought you were gone. Oh, Griffin." She allowed herself to sob against him. "But you're alive. You're here and alive."

But was her rejoicing too soon? She released him and slid away. Examined his shoulder. He repositioned himself to sit up. Swiped a hand over his eyes and face.

"I lost him. I don't know where he is." He pinned her with his gaze. "I wanted to kill him, Alice. I wanted to keep him from ever coming after you again. God help me, if that was wrong of me, I don't know. But he's the enemy here, and it didn't seem there was any other way."

"No, it's okay, you don't have to apologize. He was going to kill us both. I thought he'd killed you. Don't blame yourself—you were trying to save me."

"But I didn't save you. He could be swimming to shore right now to plan his next attack."

"I didn't want to lose anyone in this river again, but I can say I'm okay if the river took him." She rubbed her shoulders and realized where they were. Grabbed the oars again. She focused on the next set of rapids and got them through, though her hands and body shook as adrenaline drained away.

Once the raft floated in smooth water, and Alice didn't have to worry for a while, she rested, securing the oars. They'd float to Foster Bar where they could get out and get help.

"Now what?" she asked.

She'd prayed so hard for Griffin to live so that he could walk away from her again. She knew he wouldn't stay. He wasn't that kind of guy. Why did she have to fall for a man like him? Maybe she had too much wilderness in her and deep down, she didn't want a commitment, either. Maybe all these years she'd been fooling herself to think that she'd wanted Griffin to stay. And if he had stayed, or come back for her the way he'd said he would, they wouldn't be together now anyway because they were both cut from the same cloth—a piece of cloth that didn't want to be seamed together.

"What now?" she asked.

Griffin seemed to stare right through her to

the deepest part of her heart. He slid over to her. Got much too close for comfort. "I think it's time for me to do something I should have done a long time ago and take the biggest risk of my life."

She shook her head, afraid to hope at the meaning of his words. "You don't have to do anything for me, Griffin. I understand, I've always known that you weren't the kind of guy to stick around for long."

He frowned. "Shh. You're messing up the moment, Alice."

Okay.

"So what's the risk, then?"

"I want to take you away from here."

"I don't understand. What are you really saying, Griffin."

Her heart danced erratically. *Don't hope, don't hope, it can't be what you're thinking. He can't mean what you want him to mean.*

He swiped a hand down his face. "I've never had so much trouble communicating." He glanced out over the water and then back to her. "I want for us to be together…"

"Together?"

"Forever."

His words stunned her. She truly hadn't expected to hear that from him. She'd wanted to hear the words for so long and now that he actually said them, she didn't know how to react. "After everything, I don't know if I can trust you, I mean for the long term."

He nodded and hung his head. "I deserve that. I do. I own it. But please listen to me. Hear me out. Back on that beach, when he was taking you away from me, I knew if I didn't get up and if I didn't catch you, he'd take you away forever. You'd be gone from me forever. I couldn't let that happen then, and I won't let it happen now. In that moment, I realized that I ran from you, I ran from what I knew could grow between us years ago, because I was scared. You asked me before why I never came back. I was scared, Alice. You got too close. I've seen too much tragedy. I've seen unimaginable horror. I couldn't stand the thought of caring too much about someone and then losing that someone. That assignment in Kenya took me away and gave me time to think. I realized that I was damaged by everything I've seen through my camera lens. The horror, the tragedy, it all made me afraid to love you. And I had this idea that at some point I could come back to you, once I'd worked through my fear, and we'd have our chance then. Crazy I know, but when he dragged you away, I knew that I was wrong all along. I should never have imagined I could come back and you would always be there. And now, Alice… I'm more afraid of *not* loving you. I'm more afraid of letting you go, of walking away this time and losing my chance with you forever. I can't. I won't leave you again. I…love you, Alice. I love you. And I hope you can say the same."

Tears burned behind her eyes. She could hardly believe his words, but deep down, she knew they were true. She saw it in his face, in his gaze. "I love you, too."

But was his offer of love and commitment, his offer of forever, enough to secure a happy future when a madman was after her? How could they live like that, with the shadow of their experience always looming over them?

"You've traveled the world. Where could you possibly take me that I could be safe? That we could be safe? If this guy is alive, you know he'll stop at nothing to find me. I thought… I thought…that I was safe in my wilderness backyard. But if I'm not safe here, I don't know—"

Griffin snatched her to him and kissed her, cutting off her words. Oh, how she loved him. Then he released her just as quickly. "You talk too much," he said, with a teasing grin.

Her heart jumped to her throat. But he hadn't answered her question and Alice needed an answer. "Where? Where can you take me to keep me safe?"

Griffin's grin grew wider. "Right here, Alice. Right here in my arms."

EPILOGUE

Griffin stared through the lens of his camera at what would be the last of the most important series of photographs of his life—the wedding pictures. This one specifically was more like a Wilderness, Inc. reunion.

Alice would never let him forget it if he didn't get them all in—the Wilde family, brothers, wives, one proud father and Wilderness, Inc. crew who were like family anyway. Cooper and Hadley, Gray and Gemma, their father, Ethan Wilde, Olivia and Park Ranger Zachary Long, and Melanie Shore, who had been engaged to their now deceased brother Jeremy. Griffin's uncle Davis Kruse, the county sheriff, who'd stood at Griffin's side as his best man, and his mother, Jenny Slater, who flew down from Washington joined the photograph, as well.

They were a funny group of people, a tight-knit family of men and women who couldn't live or thrive anywhere except in a wilderness setting. All except his mother who preferred her home in Seattle, of course, but Griffin would join them in this.

All he had to do for the picture and for his future was take his place by Alice's side, front and center. Though he'd always loved her nature-girl look, he had to admit seeing her in that frilly wedding dress took his breath away. Made his knees weak.

"What's taking so long?" Cooper tugged at his collar with the bow tie.

"I have to get this right, so quit asking me." For the hundredth time.

Griffin could almost laugh at the scene of these rough-and-tumble men and women in formal attire, but if he did, then he'd have to pay for that indiscretion. All of them looked out of character in their fancy wedding clothes as they stood in front of the temporary gazebo set up on this beautiful spring day at a scenic spot overlooking the Rogue River.

The river that had changed his life. On that horrible day when they'd nearly been killed, he and Alice had floated on the raft until they came to the end of the Wild and Scenic portion of the river and stopped at the lodge there. Got help and told their story to his uncle once he finally resurfaced after the multiagency task force took out the marijuana operation, destroying thousands of plants and arresting a dozen armed men.

And Rafe Hanover's body finally turned up downriver, to the horror of rafting enthusiasts but to Griffin and Alice's great relief. They'd also learned the family from whom they'd borrowed the raft, along with the other rafters, had been unharmed.

But then Griffin had to face off with his greatest threat yet.

Alice's brother, Cooper Wilde.

When Griffin had made the trip back to Gideon early that morning, that sense of imminent danger still riding in his gut, he'd called and left him a message and Cooper had taken it to heart and cut his wilderness training short to come to Alice's aid, except he was too late.

Griffin and Alice had already saved each other.

When he and Alice had finally made it back to Gideon ahead of Cooper, Griffin thought Cooper would punch him in the face when he stepped out of the old, dusty Suburban and laid eyes on him.

But Alice had stood in his way. Griffin didn't need her to protect him, or stand up to her brother for him, but he'd let her explain that

Griffin had risked his life for her and that he'd then proposed.

Griffin would have given anything to have taken a picture of the shock on Cooper's face. It had taken the man six months to finally believe Griffin meant his proposal. And now, Griffin was the new official Wilderness, Inc. photographer. He'd done his part in capturing the tragedies of the world, let someone else take the reins now.

"Okay, say cheese!"

The camera was perfectly positioned on the tripod and with the seconds ticking away before it would snap the image, he joined the smiling group and took his place next to his beautiful, wilderness bride, Alice Wilde...er... Slater.

She'd always seemed part feral to him, which he loved, so it would be hard to think of her as anything but a Wilde girl. But at least she was his, all his. And right before the camera snapped, he turned and pressed his lips against hers, to capture that image forever.

* * * * *

Don't miss the other exciting stories in the
WILDERNESS, INC. *miniseries*
by Elizabeth Goddard:

TARGETED FOR MURDER
UNDERCOVER PROTECTOR
FALSE SECURITY

Find more great reads at
www.LoveInspired.com

Dear Reader,

Thank you so much for reading *Wilderness Reunion*, the final book in the *Wilderness, Inc.* series. I hope you could relate to Alice and Griffin on some level. Part of the reason for this story is I wanted to raise awareness of the devastation that's being inflicted on public lands in our beautiful country. Not only are illegal marijuana farms catastrophic to the land, the wildlife and water, but they're dangerous to people, especially nature enthusiasts as you see in this story.

In Alice's case, her world was turned upside down. She'd been minding her own business when she stumbled into some bad news—she was at the wrong place at the wrong time. Have you ever been affected by others' mistakes or "bad business"? I know I have, and though those mistakes are not anything remotely similar to the illegal marijuana farm in this story, people's bad choices have disrupted my life at times, and even changed it in big ways. There's nothing I can do about other people's actions, but for myself, I must realize how all my choices in life affect others.

Regarding our decisions, we can't know what will happen down the road, but we can always prayerfully consider our choices, and trust the One to lead and direct our path. Like Psalm 5:8 says, "Lead me, Lord, in Your righteousness because of my enemies—make Your way straight before me."

My prayer for you today is that no matter the trouble you stumble into in life, that you allow the One to direct and guide you out of it, to protect you and lead you.

I love to hear from my readers. You can connect with me on my website, Elizabeth Goddard.com, where you'll find links to my social media pages and you can also sign up for my newsletter or follow me on Bookbub!

Many blessings!
Elizabeth Goddard

Get 2 Free Books,

Plus 2 Free Gifts—

just for trying the Reader Service!

Love Inspired®

YES! Please send me 2 FREE Love Inspired® Romance novels and my 2 FREE mystery gifts (gifts are worth about $10 retail). After receiving them, if I don't wish to receive any more books, I can return the shipping statement marked "cancel." If I don't cancel, I will receive 6 brand-new novels every month and be billed just $5.24 for the regular-print edition or $5.74 each for the larger-print edition in the U.S., or $5.74 each for the regular-print edition or $6.24 each for the larger-print edition in Canada. That's a saving of at least 13% off the cover price. It's quite a bargain! Shipping and handling is just 50¢ per book in the U.S. and 75¢ per book in Canada.* I understand that accepting the 2 free books and gifts places me under no obligation to buy anything. I can always return a shipment and cancel at any time. Even if I never buy another book, the 2 free books and gifts are mine to keep forever.

Please check one:

☐ Love Inspired Romance Regular-Print
(105/305 IDN GLQC)

☐ Love Inspired Romance Larger-Print
(122/322 IDN GLQD)

Name _____ (PLEASE PRINT)

Address _____ Apt. #

City _____ State/Province _____ Zip/Postal Code

Signature (if under 18, a parent or guardian must sign)

Mail to the **Reader Service:**

IN U.S.A.: P.O. Box 1867, Buffalo, NY 14240-1867
IN CANADA: P.O. Box 611, Fort Erie, Ontario L2A 9Z9

Want to try two free books from another line?
Call 1-800-873-8635 today or visit www.ReaderService.com.

*Terms and prices subject to change without notice. Prices do not include applicable taxes. Sales tax applicable in N.Y. Canadian residents will be charged applicable taxes. Offer not valid in Quebec. This offer is limited to one order per household. Books received may not be as shown. Not valid for current subscribers to Love Inspired Romance books. All orders subject to credit approval. Credit or debit balances in a customer's account(s) may be offset by any other outstanding balance owed by or to the customer. Please allow 4 to 6 weeks for delivery. Offer available while quantities last.

Your Privacy—The Reader Service is committed to protecting your privacy. Our Privacy Policy is available online at www.ReaderService.com or upon request from the Reader Service.

We make a portion of our mailing list available to reputable third parties that offer products we believe may interest you. If you prefer that we not exchange your name with third parties, or if you wish to clarify or modify your communication preferences, please visit us at www.ReaderService.com/consumerschoice or write to us at Reader Service Preference Service, P.O. Box 9062, Buffalo, NY 14240-9062. Include your complete name and address.

LI17R

Get 2 Free Books,
Plus 2 Free Gifts—
just for trying the
Reader Service!

YES! Please send me **The Hometown Hearts Collection** in Larger Print. This collection begins with 3 FREE books and 2 FREE gifts in the first shipment. Along with my 3 free books, I'll also get the next 4 books from the Hometown Hearts Collection, in LARGER PRINT, which I may either return and owe nothing, or keep for the low price of $4.99 U.S./ $5.89 CDN each plus $2.99 for shipping and handling per shipment*. If I decide to continue, about once a month for 8 months I will get 6 or 7 more books, but will only need to pay for 4. That means 2 or 3 books in every shipment will be FREE! If I decide to keep the entire collection, I'll have paid for only 32 books because 19 books are FREE! I understand that accepting the 3 free books and gifts places me under no obligation to buy anything. I can always return a shipment and cancel at any time. My free books and gifts are mine to keep no matter what I decide.

262 HCN 3432 462 HCN 3432

Name	(PLEASE PRINT)	

Address		Apt. #

City	State/Prov.	Zip/Postal Code

Signature (if under 18, a parent or guardian must sign)

Mail to the **Reader Service**:
IN U.S.A.: P.O. Box 1867, Buffalo, NY. 14240-1867
IN CANADA: P.O. Box 609, Fort Erie, Ontario L2A 5X3

* Terms and prices subject to change without notice. Prices do not include applicable taxes. Sales tax applicable in NY. Canadian residents will be charged applicable taxes. This offer is limited to one order per household. All orders subject to approval. Credit or debit balances in a customer's account(s) may be offset by any other outstanding balance owed by or to the customer. Please allow 4 to 6 weeks for delivery. Offer available while quantities last. Offer not available to Quebec residents.

Your Privacy—The Reader Service is committed to protecting your privacy. Our Privacy Policy is available online at www.ReaderService.com or upon request from the Reader Service.

We make a portion of our mailing list available to reputable third parties that offer products we believe may interest you. If you prefer that we not exchange your name with third parties, or if you wish to clarify or modify your communication preferences, please visit us at www.ReaderService.com/consumerschoice or write to us at Reader Service Preference Service, P.O. Box 9062, Buffalo, NY. 14240-9062. Include your complete name and address.

Get 2 Free Books,

Plus 2 Free Gifts—

just for trying the
Reader Service!

LIS17R2